Flumphaderries, Flanganans and the Real Book of Bennachie

Deborah Leslie

Argo Publishing

3.5.04.

To Eilidh,

Best Wishes,

Deborah Leslie

First published in 2003 by

Argo Publishing
29 Maryfield Crescent,
Inverurie,
Aberdeenshire AB51 4RB

IBSN: 0 9546153 0 1

Printed and bound in UK by
Antony Rowe Ltd.,
Chippenham, Wiltshire

Dedication

I dedicate this book to my family and friends and to the angel of inspiration who sits on my right shoulder.

Acknowledgements

With special thanks to the following:

- Alison Tavendale, Writer in Residence, Insch, for all her advice and encouragement.
- John Blevins, for promotion work.
- Rob Ward, for Cover Design.
- Jake Wilson, for proof-reading assistance.
- My husband, Donald, for always believing in me.

Many tales have been told about the tall blue mountain range that stands guard over the North-east of Scotland. But the real story of Bennachie lies within the pages of this book: come inside and share the truth with me.

'Channel the power from another world,
Here to this place called Bennachie.
Let Haroberd's light shine clear and bright,
True Guardian of the book and key.'

Chapter One

Bennachie and Hosie's Well

"*Kirsteee... Kirsteee...*" The wind seemed to howl her name.

Kirsty MacAlister pulled the sleeves of her jacket down over her hands, shivering as her body was buffeted by the cold North-east wind. The small, dark feeling that had started in her stomach moved to tickle at the back of her neck. Reluctantly, she lifted her eyes: way above, the most easterly peak of the great blue mountain range called Bennachie stood like a giant sentry. Swirling mist cast a secretive cloak over its summit and wisps of white cloud rose from its highest point, steaming like a gigantic witches' cauldron.

"Here's where ye're hidin', lassie!"

Kirsty turned around to see her Aunt Flora bumping towards her on her red motorbike and side-car. Hosie, her black cat, sat in the side-car, his coat ruffling in the wind. Flora pulled off her crash helmet and grinned. Her face was splattered with blue paint and a disgusting drip swung from the end of her strawberry nose. She wiped it away on the back of her hand and shouted, "Ye said ye'd only be gone five minutes. I was beginnin' to think ye'd gone back to London."

Kirsty almost giggled out loud at the sight of her aunt waddling towards her: there was only one word to describe her, and that was fat. Her red hair looked as if it had never been brushed and her bulging belly shivered like a jelly inside a bright pink jumper that rode up at the front to show a pierced belly button. She wore a black leather biker jacket and matching skirt and her brown hiking boots were topped with blue woollen socks, pulled right up to meet her hairy knees.

"I...I'm sorry." Kirsty's cheeks and ears turned as red as her hair. " I needed some fresh air after the journey. I...I didn't mean to come so far."

"I canna be goin' losin' ye already, my pet." Flora put an arm around her shoulders and hugged her, her round cheeks blowing in and out as she added, "Not when we've jist found each other again."

'*Your Aunt Flora's a very successful and talented artist. And she's such a colourful character, I just know you'll have the best time.*' Kirsty sighed as her mum's voice echoed inside her head. That's what she'd said before flying off to the Mediterranean on a working holiday with her new boyfriend, Hugh. She hated Hugh. Hot tears pricked at her eyes. She blinked them away; well accustomed to being dumped with whoever would have her, she'd quickly learned that feeling sorry for herself was the biggest waste of time. Closing her eyes, she prayed that they would both get the worst sunburn ever.

"Now, Miss MacAlister," Flora pointed a fat finger at the sky, "let me introduce you to my old friend, Bennachie." She grinned and clapped her huge hands together before yelling, "Let's climb!"

"What…now? I've only just arrived." Kirsty shielded her eyes with one hand as she strained to look above her.

"Come on!" Flora, who was already on her way, turned and cupped both hands around her mouth and shouted into the wind, "Race ye to the top!"

*

Finally, standing at the summit that her Aunt Flora called 'The Mither Tap', Kirsty rested her arms on the rocky pillar of a monument. She studied the compass set in its stone face. An icy wind blew through her body, plastering her hair across her cheeks and making tears collect in the corners of her eyes. Her head swung from side to side as her gaze followed her aunt's outstretched arm, nodding as Flora pointed out villages and landmarks. And beyond the towering fir trees, farmland rolled around them: a patchwork quilt of different shades of brown and green. Fields of yellow corn rippled in a giant Mexican wave.

"It's so quiet," said Kirsty, suddenly homesick for London, for Oxford Street, with all its noise and colour. "And the sky's so dark; it's like Bennachie's afraid…like it's waiting for something to happen."

"Aye, ye're right," said Flora, leaving her side and sliding down on her big, fat behind to inspect a blackened patch in the blanket of purple heather. "It is quiet…far too quiet."

"What is this stuff?" Kirsty kicked at the pale green mist that was rising from the ground and almost covering her shoes.

"I've never seen so many bare patches in the heather," said Flora, ignoring her question. She raised her head and sniffed. "No birdsong, no bees-a-hummin': things smell bad, things smell very bad indeed."

"Stop it! You're scaring me." Kirsty jumped as a dark shape darted from between a gap in the stones before disappearing into the heather. She wrinkled her nose in disgust as a stink like rotten eggs filled the air.

"Never fear, lass." Flora took off her leather jacket and knelt on it, her socks falling down around her thick ankles. She pushed a hand inside her jumper and pulled out the chain that hung around her neck. A small silver key glinted from the palm of her hand.

The worried look left Flora's face as the smell suddenly vanished. She shoved the necklace back into her clothes and grabbed her jacket saying, "Back to the house, Kirsty. As fast as ye like."

"Catch me if you can!" Kirsty looked over her shoulder as she began her descent. The piles of boulders moved and rocked beneath her feet. She slipped and stumbled as she went.

"Whaaa!" She raced on ahead, gathering speed with every step. She laughed as she ran, her arms spinning like a windmill, loving the feeling of wide-open space and the wind against her face.

"Wow! Look at this." Kirsty skidded to a standstill and crouched down to look into a pool of water. One half was almost the same colour as the heather and the other was a grubby greenish-yellow.

"Hosie's Well," she said, reading the small wooden sign. "It's got the same name as Aunt Flora's cat." She picked a twisted stick from the path and dragged it through the water.

"No!" cried Flora, coming thundering down the slope.

"What's this?" Kirsty's eyes widened as the broken branch hit a dividing wall.

"Didn't ye hear me shoutin'? Get back!" Flora clutched at her sides, gasping for breath. She pushed Kirsty in the chest and grabbed the stick from her hand, sending it hurling through the air.

Kirsty sat back on the edge of the path and watched as her aunt dropped to her knees. She flattened the grass with both hands and peered down into the well.

"What's happening?" Kirsty crawled over and joined Flora. She leaned towards her reflection and took a deep breath as a gust of wind sent ripples out across the whole pool. As she watched, the left-hand side of the well began to smoke and glow with a pale green light. She covered her nose and mouth with her hand as the same vile stench that she'd noticed earlier rose from its depths.

Flora sat down with a thump on a rock. She held her head in her hands for a moment before getting to her feet and hurrying down the steep slope.

"Is something wrong?" Kirsty sprinted to catch up with her aunt as they reached the bottom.

"*Mmm. Mmm.* No time to waste. *Mmm. Mmm.*" Flora hummed and muttered to herself as she strode along, her rough red arms swinging by her sides, her enormous rear jiggling up and down as she went.

"Jump into Scarlet, lass, an' save yer legs." Flora threw a pudding-bowl crash helmet into Kirsty's arms. "Let's ride!" She gave a loud whoop as she kick-started her motorbike into action.

Kirsty pulled on the ridiculous-looking helmet and clambered into the side-car. She moved over as Hosie jumped in beside her, pushing to find a space on Scarlet's shiny red seat. The smell of leather and petrol inside the side-car made her feel sick as they gathered speed, kicking up clouds of dust as they roared along the road which led back to Benderrie Manor. She closed her eyes and blushed as she remembered that morning and her embarrassment when her aunt had picked her up at Aberdeen airport in the bright red contraption.

Chapel of Weerdee

The sign flashed in front of Kirsty's eyes. A bald man wearing a red-and-white striped apron was spitting on a rag and polishing the wooden signposts that had been hammered into the grass verge. She read out loud from them as they rode into the village:

Come along to -
Weerdee Village Fair.
This Saturday at 2 o'clock
Everyone welcome!

Kirsty's head twisted from side to side, taking in the sights and smells as they rode through the village square. She could see a few small shops, one lonely-looking dog and three villagers going about their business. A scrumptious smell of warm bread floated from the door of a café and mingled with the pungent pong from a tractor and muck-spreader that was parked across the street.

They slowed down as they passed a white building on the outskirts of the village. Children were running around inside what looked like a wire cage, screaming and shouting at the tops of their voices.

"That's oor wee school," shouted Flora, "an' it looks like it's play-time."

"Ow! Your claws are sharp." Kirsty pushed Hosie's paws off her knee as Scarlet climbed up the hill, leaving the village behind. She felt an unexpected shiver run along her spine as she was bounced up and down inside the side-car; Hosie had turned to stare straight at some strange statues which were standing in a clearing in the woods. They were covered in a thick layer of green moss and she watched them over one shoulder as they turned into the end of the gravel drive that led to Flora's house.

"Home sweet home." Flora tugged at the leather chin-strap and pulled off her helmet as they shuddered to a standstill.

Chapter 2

Benderrie Manor and the Forbidden Room

Benderrie Manor sat grimly against the sky-line like a grey cardboard cut-out, its rows of narrow windows glittering like the black slits of watchful eyes. Kirsty screamed as Hosie jumped onto her lap, digging his claws into her leg. He sat up straight and tilted his head to one side as if he had heard something, then sprang from the side-car and ran towards a circle of standing stones which loomed from the field at the side of the house.

*

"Wipe yer feet and close the door behind ye," said Flora.

"Wow!" Kirsty clamped a hand over her mouth as she looked around the wood-panelled entrance hall: a full suit of armour stood in the far corner and behind the front door was an umbrella stand made from an elephant's foot. A life-sized figure of a wild-eyed tribesman with a mad grin on his face leaned up against one of the walls. Near the bottom of the staircase stood a stuffed brown bear. Its yellow glass eyes seemed to follow her and its long teeth hung over a black bottom lip that was stretched and shiny.

"Dinna worry yerself about the wildlife, Kirsty." Flora held her sides as she began to laugh. "They've jist been fed." She stretched up, pulled a black-barrelled rifle from the wall and pretended to take aim at the bear. "Yer Great-Grandfather was a big game hunter. He travelled the world in search o' these beauties."

Kirsty's footsteps echoed in her ears as she walked into the centre of the tiled floor.

Wrinkling her nose at the damp, musty smell, she tilted her head back to look up at the ceiling. Ropes of grey cobwebs stretched between a huge chandelier and the antlers on the head of a cross-eyed stag.

"Excuse the dust," shouted Flora, disappearing through an archway. "No matter how much I clean this place, it jist seems to get dirtier by the day."

Kirsty's gaze dropped to take in the rest of the house. A rickety banister ran all the way around the first and second floors. *One. Two. Three. Four. Five. Six*…she rubbed her eyes, losing count of how many doors she could see through the spindles of the banister.

"Come on, Kirsty!"

The sound of Flora's voice startled Kirsty. She climbed the three stone steps that led up to the arch and peered down a dimly lit hall: there were portraits of all shapes and sizes as far as she could see.

She blinked as her eyes became accustomed to the gloom. Alongside a huge oil painting of Bennachie stood a life-size portrait of three little girls. They all wore summer outfits, their pale faces framed with long red hair. The smallest of the girls held a big brown book against the skirt of her pink polka-dot dress.

Kirsty jumped as her Aunt Flora appeared behind her and put an arm around her waist.

"Do ye recognise any o' these lovely lassies?" she asked, pressing a hand between Kirsty's shoulder blades and pushing her closer to the picture.

"Is that you, Aunt Flora?" Kirsty pointed at the child with the round face and chubby arms and legs. She wore a white cardigan and a yellow skirt, covered with tiny orange-centred daisies.

"Aye, that's me." Flora slapped the backs of her hands against her double chin. "I've always been a bit on the sturdy side."

Kirsty felt a blush warm her cheeks and turned her attentions back towards the painting. "The girl in the navy-and-white checked pinafore - that's Mum!" she said, covering her mouth with a hand and giggling. "She looked even grumpier then than she does now."

Flora laughed and nodded.

Kirsty gasped, shocked at what she saw next. "The little one's eyes…" she touched her face, "they're like mine. One blue and one green."

"Ye've got extra-special eyes." Flora crouched down so that their faces were almost touching. "An' now ye know where they come from."

"But who is she?"

"Elvira." Flora patted Kirsty's cheek with her great sausage fingers and whispered, "My wee sister Elvira."

"I didn't know you had another sister. Why didn't Mum ever say?"

"Och, she was always jealous o' us." Flora's eyes danced and her red face lit up at the memory. "We were forever up to somethin'. Harriet was the oldest...I suppose she felt left out."

"I've always wanted a sister - or even a brother would do." Kirsty sighed. "If Mum had stayed in Scotland, I could've had a real family. Why did she have to move away?"

"It was a terrible time," said Flora, taking a deep breath. "Both yer Grandparents had already died, an' then when Harriet decided she had to move all the way to London to pursue her wonderful career in Interior Design, it nearly broke my heart."

"I can't even remember having a dad." Kirsty felt hot tears rush to her eyes. "Mum said he ran away and left us 'cos he hated London."

Flora just tutted in reply and gave her a sympathetic look. "I asked her to send photographs," she said, blinking her watery eyes, "but she never did get around to it."

Kirsty watched as a tear ran down her aunt's cheek. "You were only six months old an' such a bonny wee thing. Partin' with you so soon after losin' Elvira an' her family was almost more than I could bear." She scrubbed at her face with the palms of her hands and swung around to point at a framed wedding portrait of her younger sister and her handsome, dark-haired husband.

"What happened to her?" Kirsty leaned forward and studied Elvira's smiling face. The bride looked so happy, and she could almost smell the pink roses in her hair.

"We all lived together in this house..." Flora paused and looked straight at Kirsty, "until the day she left us...Elvira, her husband Charlie an' their lovely baby Roanna..." Her face crumpled as if the memory was too painful. "Eleven years ago - that's the last time I spoke to her."

"But you must have tried to look for them?" Kirsty stared into her aunt's wet eyes.

"Och! My dear, sweet lassie," Flora patted her head and smiled, "all the lookin' in the world won't bring them back. I've jist had to content myself with watchin'...an' waitin'," she added, mysteriously.

Kirsty's gaze moved back to the painting of the blue mountain. The feeling of fear that she'd experienced earlier came back to her now as she stared at the picture.

"I didn't tell you before," said Kirsty, "but...Bennachie looks just like the mountain that I see in my dreams. I...I've dreamed of this place all of my life." She laughed then, feeling suddenly foolish.

"I always knew that ye'd come back." Flora nodded as if she understood. "An' it's not a minute too soon. I asked Harriet to send you last week," she added, twisting her mouth disapprovingly, "but she was too busy to organise a flight."

"She's *always* too busy. The only time we talk is when she drives me to school," said Kirsty with a sigh.

"Do ye like yer school?"

"I hate it! Some of the girls tease me about my red hair and my different coloured eyes. I...I'm not that popular."

"Well, Kirsty MacAlister, ye're popular here," said Flora, slipping an arm around her shoulders as they went back into the entrance hall. "Odd eyes an' red hair are all the rage."

Kirsty wiped her eyes and smiled at her aunt.

"So what are ye waitin' for? Go on! Explore!" bellowed Flora, walking into a kitchen, with a long wooden table, a roaring red fire and a whitewashed wall full of big brass pots and pans. "Make yerself at home."

Kirsty climbed the polished wooden stairs that rose from the middle of the great hall and found that almost all the rooms on the top floor of the house were either empty or piled high with cardboard boxes and rubbish. One of the smaller rooms had been turned into an artist's studio. Half-finished pencil sketches and oil paintings leaned against wobbly wooden easels and crusty tubes of paint oozed worms of different colours. A big jam jar of cloudy water held all Flora's paintbrushes.

"Ten minutes, Kirsty!" Flora's voice came winding up the stairs. "Dinner's nearly ready - it's home-made beef stew followed by trifle."

"Great! I'm starving." The banister gave a loud creak as Kirsty leaned against it. She smiled down at her aunt, who was brandishing a big wooden spoon in the air. Her stomach made a loud groaning noise as a scrumptious smell of cooking wafted up to where she stood.

Back on the first floor, Kirsty pushed open door after door. There were huge four-poster beds, lumpy antique sofas, a library filled to the ceiling with dusty leather-bound books and even a music-room with a walnut-brown grand piano. She looked through window after window, the strangely familiar view of Bennachie seeming to fill every peeling frame.

Kirsty blinked. *Was it her imagination?* It looked like a pale green light was coming from beneath one of the doors at the end of the corridor. The stripe of colour escaped and curled upwards into a white-tipped smoky finger that seemed to be beckoning her. She took a deep breath as she reached the last room on the landing.

Her fingers trembled as she slid back the shiny bolt, her other hand closing around the brass knob. The door groaned on its hinges as it swung open.

The light disappeared as soon as Kirsty stepped into the room. She looked around. In one corner was a four-poster bed with the covers rolled down as if someone had just got up, and in the other was a child's wooden cot with two dusty feeding bottles on a stool by its side. A book lay open on the bedside cabinet. Clothes hung over chairs, and a pair of red tartan slippers sat neatly by the bed. A dirt-encrusted rocker that wasn't allowed to rock was silhouetted against a window which was taller and wider than any of the others in the house. Two blocks of wood were wedged beneath the runners of the stricken seat and a big black spider scuttled between the webs that stretched from spindle to spindle.

Crossing the room, she stopped in front of the dusty dressing-table and ran a hand over a silver-backed mirror and comb. The brush lay upside down and long red hairs were wound through its bristles.

Kirsty stared at her reflection. Her own odd eyes looked back at her, her freckled face looking paler than usual against her red hair. She jumped and spun around as the bedroom door banged against the wall.

"What are ye doin' in here?" Flora stood with a horrified expression on her face, the palms of her hands pressed against her fat cheeks.

"You said I could explore. And…and I thought I could see something…" Kirsty stared down at the faded carpet and tried to hide her tears.

"It's my fault, lass. I should've told ye not to open the bolted door." Flora pulled her back into the passageway. She shot the lock back into place before holding up the silver key that hung around her neck. Her face was flushed and she was breathing heavily as she said, "It's jist that I dinna use this room anymore."

"But it's full of clothes…and someone's things."

"Please…jist leave it, Kirsty. I've got my reasons. An' this room is out of bounds. Understand?"

Kirsty nodded.

"You'll be sleeping at the other end of the corridor, right next to me. Come on, lass!" She poked Kirsty in the stomach and crooked a fat finger in the air as she began to walk away. "Let's get some good Scots food inside that skinny little belly o' yours." She turned and smiled as she added, "And then it's off to bed for you, my dearie: ye dinna want to be late for yer first day at Weerdee School."

Kirsty looked down. The glowing green light was back, even brighter than before. She felt her whole body tense as another ghostly finger separated itself and snaked across the passageway. It seemed to stop for a moment, as if making up its mind, before turning and winding itself around her ankles. Kirsty felt a mixture of fear and fascination as she looked down at her legs. She opened her mouth to scream then shut it again as the light turned and disappeared under the locked door.

Not daring to look behind, Kirsty ran along the landing and down the stairs, jumping over the last four steps that took her back onto the ground floor. She bent her head as she passed the portrait gallery, carefully avoiding the watchful eyes of the three little sisters.

*

Exhausted by the climb and the excitement of the day, Kirsty stretched her body to fit her bed. The metal frame creaked and groaned under her weight. Tugging at the heavy patchwork quilt, she turned onto her side. She tucked her knees up under her chin and watched as the moon made strange, scary-looking shapes on the bedroom walls. Then, closing her eyes tightly, she did what she always did when she was afraid; she began to recite a little rhyme inside her head:

Ordinary objects transform without light,
Normal by day but fearsome by night.
A big pile of clothes change shape in the chair -
It's the devil himself with teeth like a bear.

A scream stuck in Kirsty's throat as a weight landed on her feet. She pulled the covers right up over her head, hardly daring to breathe as the thing on the bottom of the bed began to move around. Slowly, her heart hammering hard inside her chest, she peeped over the edge of the quilt. She felt her whole body tense - then she saw Hosie the black cat coming towards her.

Her breath still came in little gasps and her hand shook as she stretched out to stroke him. Hosie pushed the dark triangle of his face against her arm then draped his warm body across her lap. She smiled and tickled his silky underbelly. His eyelids flickered and Kirsty felt her mouth fall open with shock when she saw that his eyes were pink. And when he brought his head close to hers, she was sure that she saw him smile. Except that she knew cats didn't smile.

Chapter Three

Chapel of Weerdee School

"Chapel of Weerdee Primary School," said Kirsty, as she read the sign on the wall. She chewed on her bottom lip and twisted the strap on her bag as she watched the other children stream inside.

The headmistress stared through the glass double doors for a moment before coming out to meet her. "You must be Miss MacAlister," she said, the tendons on her scrawny neck standing out like lengths of twisted pink rope as she nodded her head. "Your aunt told me to expect you."

Kirsty watched as her thin lips drew back in a smile, showing a line of discoloured teeth that leaned towards each other like the circle of stones beside Benderrie Manor. The teacher's black hair was pleated into a long, shiny snake. Her nose was very long and four huge, pus-filled spots throbbed on her chin. The darkest eyes imaginable glittered from beneath a crooked fringe.

"I'm new here myself." The headmistress bent her pipe-cleaner body to look Kirsty in the face. "Maybe we can help each other."

"Yes, Miss. Miss..." Kirsty pulled away from the dreadful smelling draught that blew from the teacher's open mouth.

"The name's Knowall." The headmistress put a bony finger beneath her chin and came so close that Kirsty could see her own face reflected in the ebony eyes. "*Miss* Knowall to you."

"So how are you liking Benderrie Manor?" Miss Knowall's fingers dug into Kirsty's neck as she steered her along the polished corridor.

"It's big." Kirsty hung her head. "And kind of scary."

"In what way?" Miss Knowall stopped walking and put both of her hard hands on Kirsty's shoulders.

"It's nothing really." Kirsty stared at the floor, struggling to find the right words. "It's more of a kind of bad..."

"A bad feeling," suggested Miss Knowall, raising her thin eyebrows. "Like something's about to happen?"

“Yes. That’s right.” Kirsty lifted her head to look at her teacher. “How did you know?”

The headmistress smiled then, a funny smile that didn’t quite reach her eyes. And then she started to laugh. Her mean lips peeled back to reveal all her teeth and she snorted and cackled until Kirsty could see the funny wobbly bit at the back of her throat. She slapped a hand against Kirsty’s back and shoved her into the classroom.

“Good morning, Miss Knowall!” The children spoke as one.

“Girls and boys.” The headmistress clapped her hands together. “We have a new girl. Say hello to Kirsty MacAlister.”

“Hello.” The pupils shuffled in their seats.

“Sit!” snapped Miss Knowall, pushing Kirsty towards a table.

She blushed as she pulled out a red plastic chair.

“Open your books.” The headmistress tapped her ruler against the long line of her nose.

Kirsty turned to the fair-haired boy who was sitting next to her.

“Hi!” he whispered. “I’m Brodie.” His brown eyes looked huge behind his thick glasses and when he smiled he showed a shiny train-track brace.

She smiled back at him before looking at the girl who sat across from her: she had a white face, and the blackest hair that she had ever seen. The girl gave her a shy look before saying, “And I’m Jane.”

“Hi, Jane!” Kirsty grinned as their eyes met.

“Now then you lot!” Miss Knowall clapped her hands again. “I’m hoping that we can devote most of the day to making our final preparations for tomorrow’s Village Fair.” Her cheeks flushed red and she looked excited as she cracked the knuckles on both of her bony hands. “As you’ll all know, my good self and the generous shopkeepers of Weerdee are organising and sponsoring the whole event. Oh yes! YES!” The headmistress’s voice became louder and louder and her dark eyes glistened. “It’s going to be wonderful - a day to remember.”

“But for now,” said Miss Knowall, her tone returning to normal, “let’s get on with some work. You…I forget your name.” She pointed at Brodie. “We were discussing the environment and the changes that we can see around us. Read from your work."

Kirsty watched as Brodie opened his homework book. He blinked nervously behind his glasses as he began to speak.

Miss Knowall leaned back in her chair. She chewed on one of her long yellow fingernails as she listened. Suddenly, the slits of her beady black eyes snapped wide open. She spat a sliver of nail out across the floor and held up a hand. "STOP! Stop right there." She moved to stand in front of the small-paned window. "Read that bit again."

Kirsty's eyes followed Miss Knowall as she looked out at Bennachie. She sucked on the end of her pencil; wherever you went, the mountain seemed to follow. Yesterday, it had seemed dark and sinister, but this morning it looked beautiful, watery yellow sunlight lighting up its purple slopes.

"I said, read it again!" snapped Miss Knowall, spinning around to face her pupils.

"My…my Gran is worried about some of the changes on Bennachie." Brodie took a deep breath. "Strange things are happening."

"Go on! Go on." Miss Knowall rolled her pencil between her horrible teeth.

"Well, she's seen some extra big bluebottles and frogs and spiders and stuff running about. She's noticed lots of dead patches in the heather and…green mist and some really rotten smells. And she says that the water from the burns is dark and not as clean as it used to be."

"Good. Good." Miss Knowall looked over her shoulder at Bennachie. "I mean…that's a very good observation."

Kirsty felt a creepy sensation run through her body when the headmistress wound her long arms around her skinny frame and seemed to give herself a little hug of excitement.

Briiiiiing. Kirsty jumped as the bell for interval rang. She pulled a bag of crisps from her rucksack and joined the line of kids that snaked out of the classroom and into the playground.

Kirsty sniffed as she stepped outside; she could smell the same stink that she'd noticed on the slopes of Bennachie. And for a moment, she thought that she could see a low cloud of the creeping green mist that had covered her shoes blowing over the ground. She rubbed her eyes and when she looked again, it was gone.

The playground was quite big with a rusty metal fence running all the way around it. The kids were charging around, pulling at each other's coats and chatting and screaming with laughter. Jane was sitting by herself on the wall watching some girls skipping and Brodie was standing in a line waiting to be picked for a game of football.

"Get lost, Brodie!" shouted one of the boys. "We dinna need you in oor team."

"That's big Bogie Burnett," whispered Jane. "He's the school bully."

Bogie Burnett was at least a head and shoulders taller than any of the other boys and he had a mouth to match. Both of his nostrils were encrusted with bright green bogies and two slimy candles of snot slid up and down when he spoke.

"Are ye deef as well as stupid?" Bogie Burnett's tongue flicked at the lime-green channels on his top lip. He sniffed loudly before wiping his nose on his sleeve.

Brodie looked as if he was about to cry, then pulled a blue inhaler out of his pocket. He shook it and took two puffs before joining Jane on the wall.

Kirsty felt a stab of sympathy for Brodie and ran over and sat down between him and Jane.

"Bad asthma, huh?" She gave him a smile.

"Yep. Asthma, glasses, brace, I've got the lot." He tapped his specs and turned his bottom lip inside out to show off his metal-work before adding, "I'm a total wreck."

"I widna sit with us," said Jane, pulling the sleeves of a coat that was far too small for her, down over her skinny white arms. "We're the sickly ones."

"What's wrong with you?" Kirsty turned to look at her.

"It's my heart." She unwrapped a sticky-looking red and yellow lollipop and stuck it in her mouth. "I take loads o' tablets - an' I'm waitin' for an operation." The white stick of the strawberry and custard flavour lolly wiggled up and down as she spoke. "My Auntie Nell says I'm nae allowed to run around."

"What's it got to do with her?" Kirsty moved closer to Jane.

"She hisna got a dad and her mum cleared off withoot her," explained Brodie, between mouthfuls of a big green apple. "She's livin' at her auntie's."

"I haven't got a dad either." Kirsty smiled at Jane and then at Brodie. "I've got a mum, but she likes me to call her Harriet. She's a *designer* and she never has any time for me. All she does is work, work, work. And then when she's not doing that, she has her friends over to the house and they sit around all afternoon drinking sherry and eating silly little cucumber sandwiches with the crusts cut off."

Kirsty opened her crisps and sniffed at them. "Want one?" she asked, holding out the bag. Brodie and Jane smiled and shuffled along the wall so that their shoulders were touching. They sat munching noisily on the cheese and onion crisps, their three sets of legs swinging in time.

"She's such a fuss-pot too," said Kirsty suddenly. "I'm not allowed to eat anything with my fingers. I must *never* drop my 'h's when I talk. And I always have to say 'fluff' instead of 'fart'."

She watched as Brodie and Jane looked at each other then began to laugh, soggy crisp crumbs spraying from their open mouths. Kirsty joined in and didn't even care when Bogie Burnett and his gang stopped what they were doing and turned to stare at them.

*

Back in the classroom, Miss Knowall dumped a pile of coloured paper on the middle of the table. She banged down a box with scissors and glue and shouted, "Let's have some decorations then, you scruffy lot."

The rest of the day flew by in a sticky flurry of paper chain-making and endless wrapping of small parcels of sweets, pencils and rubbers for the Lucky Dip barrels. Kirsty's fingers ached and she was glad when the bell rang. Reaching under her desk, she picked up her rucksack.

"Just a minute, Miss MacAlister." Miss Knowall's pointy black shoes click-clacked against the wooden floor.

Kirsty could see her knobbly knees through the legs of the table. "Yes, Miss?" She sat up straight in her chair, clutching her bag tightly against her chest.

"I just wondered if you'd had much of a chance to explore your new home?" Miss Knowall smiled and brought her face down close to her own.

"No...not really." Kirsty's voice shook as she looked into the black holes of the teacher's eyes. "I only arrived yesterday, and it's *so* big."

"Well, just remember, your aunt's house is one of the oldest in the district. So, if you find anything *unusual* which you think could be of interest to the class, please feel free to bring it along to the school-house," she smiled, showing all her teeth again, "at any time - night or day."

"Like what?" Kirsty shrank back; the headmistress was so close now that she could feel her hot, smelly breath on her face.

"Well now. Let me think." Miss Knowall crossed the room and peered out through the window. "I'm very interested in books." Her long nose almost touched the glass. "Particularly antique hardbacks: ones with lots of illustrations."

Kirsty didn't look back as she walked away from the school. She hadn't liked the scary way that Miss Knowall had looked at her when she'd said that she liked old books. And she could still feel her eyes staring after her as she began to run, her schoolbag bumping off her hip and her red hair flying out behind her, like a banner in the wind.

She stopped running as she came to the Village Square; strings of bunting for the Fair were hanging across the main street, tiny triangles of red, yellow, blue and green fluttering in the breeze. She gazed through one of the small shop windows, licking her lips at the sight of all the treats: long, pink-and-white striped candy sticks, chocolate bars, all flavours of bubble gum and row upon row of different kinds of sweets in gigantic screw top jars.

Kirsty searched in the pocket of her coat and found her purse. The brass bell above the sweet shop door jangled as she stepped into the shop.

Chapter Four

The Shopkeepers

"I haven't seen you before. Are you from the Manor?" The shopkeeper leaned across the counter and stared at Kirsty. Her straw-coloured hair was pulled into a tight bun and small eyes, like a mole's, flickered behind thick, black-rimmed glasses.

Kirsty nodded. "Do you know my Aunt Flora?" she asked, unzipping her purse.

"No. I'm new here too." The woman gave a thin-lipped smile. "But I know of her." She reached across the wooden counter and poked the sharp point of her pencil into Kirsty's forehead. "You've got the odd eyes!" A shower of spit sprayed from her bottom lip and landed on the back of Kirsty's hand. "Just like Elvira."

Kirsty wiped her hand on her jeans and backed away, saying, "I thought you were new here?"

"Oh, I am. I am." The woman gave her a sly look. "But I do keep my eyes and my ears open. I suggest that you do the same."

Kirsty gripped the strap of her schoolbag as the assistant began to laugh. Her eyes widened in horror as her mouth opened to reveal dark yellow teeth. *They're just like Miss Knowall's,* she thought, pushing her purse into her pocket and reaching for the door handle.

Her mouth was dry and her heart was racing as she stood with her back pressed up against the shop door. She gave a long whistle of relief at the welcome sight of her Aunt Flora coming thundering across the village square.

"Yoohoo!" Flora held her battered shopping basket high in the air. "Yooohooo!"

Kirsty gave her a shaky smile.

"What's up with the bonniest lass in Weerdee?" Flora's three chins wobbled as she spoke.

"Nothing." Kirsty shook her head "Nothing at all."

"Are ye sure?" Flora twisted her big red lips, the long line of her eyebrows disappearing under her fringe like one giant ginger caterpillar.

"I'm certain." Kirsty managed a smile. "Sure as can be."

"Right then." A satisfied Flora waved her shopping list in front of Kirsty's face. "I've been to the baker's an' the butcher's." She paused for a moment. "Ye know, everyone who used to own those businesses has sold up an' moved on, an' all within the last few weeks." She pushed open the sweet shop door with her shoulder. "Come on. Ye can choose whatever ye like."

Back inside the shop, Kirsty carefully avoided the assistant's eye.

"So you're the new owner." Kirsty's aunt's fat face creased with her smile. "I live up at Benderrie Manor. The name's Flora."

"Mrs Sookhard." The shopkeeper shot out a hand tipped with yellow nails that curled over at the ends.

Kirsty watched as Flora shook her hand before plonking her ancient wicker basket on the counter.

"What's happened to old Mrs Henderson?" she asked. "Maybe ye could give me her new address?"

"Didn't leave an address."

"*Arrr. Mm... Mmm. Grrrr.*"

Mrs Sookhard turned her attentions to an old-fashioned carriage pram that was coming trundling through on its own from the direction of the shop's storeroom. The thin, high-pitched grizzle rose from under a mountain of grubby-looking blankets.

"Right then!" She tutted impatiently, then clamped a scrawny, blue-veined hand around the carriage's rusty handle. "Can I get you something? Or have you just come in for the chat?"

"I...I'll jist take a wee bag o' sherbet lemons." Flora pointed to a jar on the shelf.

"Waaa. *Grrr...*WAAAAA!" The cry became louder and more insistent.

Kirsty gasped as Mrs Sookhard began to bounce the pram so hard that the baby inside jumped up and down in the air.

"Here you go," she said, unscrewing the lid from the sweet jar and throwing a sherbet lemon at the tot. "Get your gums round that."

"It'll choke!" Kirsty cried. "Babies can't eat..."

Flora and Kirsty's mouths fell open as a small hand appeared and picked the sweet from the crocheted cover. There was a moment's silence followed by a furious crunching.

Kirsty almost screamed as the black-eyed baby sat up; it had to be the ugliest child that she had ever seen.

"Oh my!" A look of absolute amazement passed over Flora's face as the infant began to laugh, showing a row of yellow teeth. Dark hair, which looked like a wig, stuck out from its head at odd angles.

"Oh my!" repeated Flora. "What a... what a bonny baby."

Kirsty shuddered as the child suddenly fell back. She held her breath for a moment then turned to see her Aunt Flora's astonished gaze as a deep sigh of satisfaction rose from the depths of the pram.

The assistant tipped the sweets from a giant glass jar. They rattled as they fell onto the brass scales.

"So," Flora's voice trembled slightly as she spoke, "how are ye settlin' into Weerdee?"

The shopkeeper ignored her question and shook the bright yellow sweets into a paper bag.

"I used to know all the shopkeepers," Flora continued. "An' now, I hardly recognise a soul."

"That'll be right." Mrs Sookhard gave a small twist of a smile. "Things are certainly changing around here - lots of new blood in the village."

"Oh! An' this is my niece, Kirsty," said Flora, fumbling in her purse. "Well, say hello then!" She tutted and looked embarrassed when Kirsty didn't speak.

"Cat got your tongue?" The woman behind the counter winked.

"We've already met," said Kirsty politely.

The shopkeeper gave a friendly smile that showed no trace of her earlier unpleasantness. Kirsty watched as she swept a yellow fingernail around the white-powdered bowl of the scales, then licked the sherbet from its tip.

"She's a strange one," said Flora, popping a sweet in Kirsty's mouth as they left the shop.

Another weirdo in Weerdee, thought Kirsty, sucking on the sour treat as she followed her aunt. She smiled to herself at the mesmerizing sight of Flora's ample behind filling the narrow pavement and banging from side to side as she steamed along.

Kirsty looked back at the sweet shop just in time to see Mrs Sookhard crossing the village square. She moved quickly and silently, taking little steps as she ran.

"Who are *they*?" Kirsty pulled at her aunt's sleeve and nodded towards where Mrs Sookhard stood in a huddle with two other people.

"Now, jist let me think for a minute, lass." Flora's brow furrowed as she struggled to remember. "Yes! Yes...I've got it." She pointed past Mrs Sookhard to the man by her side. "That's Mr Savage the butcher an' the one with the frizzy grey hair, that's..." she clicked her fingers in the air, "Mrs...Mrs Hardpiece and her pet pig Gristle." Flora nodded across the road towards a café with green-and-white checked curtains. "She's taken over the '*Rumbly-Tum*' tearoom and bakery shop."

Kirsty shuddered at the sight of the shopkeepers. Each was as unattractive as the other.

Gristle the big pot-bellied pig snorted and grunted, bubbles of snot blowing from his black snout. Mrs Hardpiece pulled at his chain then whispered something in the butcher's ear, who wiped his hands on his bloodstained apron before throwing back his shiny bald head and laughing.

"I don't like the look of them one bit," she whispered. "They're giving me the creeps. They all look so...so *weird*."

This time it was Mrs Sookhard's turn to laugh. Kirsty wasn't sure if the sweet shop owner and her companions had overheard their conversation or not. But as she turned towards them, they all smiled and waved.

"Come on!" Flora raised her hand then walked on. "Let's get back to the Manor."

Kirsty almost choked on her sherbet lemon when she looked back at the shopkeepers. They stood in a line, their sharp little eyes looking her up and down. And as they grinned, they showed three sets of matching yellow teeth.

Chapter Five

Into the Painting

Kirsty twisted and turned and tried her hardest to fall asleep.

"Grunt-*wheeeee*. Grunt-*wheeeee*." The sound of Flora's snoring seemed to shake the wall between the rooms.

She put her hands over her ears and then wrapped her pillow around her head to block out the noise.

"*Kirsteee... Kirsteee...*" She listened as the same voice that had called her name at the bottom of Bennachie joined in with her aunt's breathing. The cry became louder and louder, so loud that it seemed as if it had crept into bed beside her.

"It... it's only the wind," said Kirsty, as the noise suddenly subsided.

The room was silent now apart from a loud growl of hunger from Kirsty's stomach. She swung her bare feet onto the wooden floor, pulled on her dressing-gown and went out into the corridor.

Kirsty poked her head around the edge of her aunt's bedroom door: Flora was lying flat on her back, snoring away like a huge, red-faced elephant, her fleshy lips vibrating with every breath. She had the blankets pulled up tightly under her chin with her flabby feet sticking out from the bottom. Kirsty covered her mouth with both hands and tried not to laugh.

Still giggling to herself, she made her way down to the kitchen. But with every step she took, a small fearful feeling grew inside her belly. "Look straight ahead," she said out loud as she began to run. "Not to the side or behind. Especially not behind!"

*

With one hand clutching a glass of milk and the other holding a massive strawberry jam sandwich, Kirsty bolted back up the stairs. She breathed a sigh of relief as she stood outside her bedroom door; she'd got back safely, and by the noises coming from Flora's direction, she hadn't been missed.

"*Kirsteee...*" She swallowed hard as the wind howled her name again. The glass of milk and the sandwich fell against the carpet with a dull thud. She held her breath, praying that the noise wouldn't wake her aunt.

"*KIRSTEEE...*" It seemed even louder than before. Kirsty dragged her eyes away from the puddle of milk and turned towards the voice, knowing that it was coming from the last room on the corridor. She wasn't sure how she knew. She just did. And although she was afraid she walked towards it.

Kirsty summoned all her courage and closed her fingers around the brass doorknob of the forbidden room. It squeaked as it turned. She found the light switch just as the door closed behind her with a sharp click. Her face and the palms of her hands were soaked with sweat and she could feel her pulse beating against her throat as she crossed the floor. She sneezed; the carpet was so dirty she could see the imprints of her bare feet in the dust.

Kirsty stopped in her tracks - the old rocking-chair that stood in front of the window was glowing with a ghostly green light. She stared at her white-faced reflection in the black gap between the curtains before sitting down on the seat's dusty velvet cushion.

She sat quite still for a moment, her hands resting on the rocker's cobwebbed arms. Holding her breath, she leaned over and kicked away the blocks of wood that were jammed beneath the runners. And then she began to rock.

Kirsty screamed as the room seemed to burst into life. Faster and faster she went. The lights went on and off and the tartan slippers rose into the air and slapped their soles together. The book on the bedside table opened then closed with a thump, clouds of dust rising from between its pages. On and on they went: *Slap. Thump. Slap. Thump.*

Kirsty shrieked as the chair suddenly stopped rocking and catapulted her across the room and onto the dressing-table stool. She watched in horror as the silver-backed mirror, brush, and comb slid back towards an old jewellery box with a broken lock. An invisible finger began to draw on the dusty space where they had been. "*K-I-R-S-T-Y*" She spelled out the letters which made up her name.

Kirsty raised her head and saw the look of terror reflected on her face as she heard something which made all the hairs at the back of her neck stand to attention: a scratching sound was coming from inside the dressing-table. She wiped the sweat from her top lip. There it was again: *scritch, scratch, scratch, scritch.*

Kirsty stood up and backed away, knocking over the pink-padded seat. She shook her head and plugged her ears with her fingers as the noise seemed to fill every corner of the room.

"STOP!" Kirsty covered her eyes with her hands, and began to recite one of her favourite little rhymes:

"*Silly Miss Imagination,*
Made it happen in her head.
Silly Miss Imagination -
Forget your dreams and go to bed."

The scratching noise stopped. Kirsty slowly parted her fingers and walked towards the dressing-table. She picked up the stool and sat back down. For a moment, nothing happened. And then…

She watched in amazement as the top two drawers slid open and the mirror began to glow with an eerie green light. Leaning forward, she peered at her reflection and screwed up her nose at the terrible smell like rotten eggs that seemed to be seeping up through the floorboards.

Kirsty yelled and jumped into the air as the mirror was suddenly filled with row upon row of furry, rat-like countenances, their yellow teeth chattering up and down, their red eyes staring at her. She fell back against the bed as more faces shot out from the top two drawers. And as they opened their mouths, a stream of something gluey and black flew through the air, covering her head and shoulders like a sticky spider's web. Kirsty clawed at her cheeks and hair as the creatures began to laugh.

Her mouth dropped open in shock as the third and bottom drawer slid silently open. A brilliant white light with a glowing lilac centre streamed out and a sweet smell of flowers filled the air. There was a loud bang as the glass cracked before shattering into a million pieces. The vile little beasts screeched and thrashed around furiously before disappearing into the depths of the dressing-table.

Kirsty gasped, her breath coming in great gulps as she stared at the broken glass sprayed over the floor like little sharp-edged diamonds. Clearing a space, she dropped to her knees and peered inside the bottom drawer.

Its base seemed to have turned to liquid, shining and glowing as it swirled. Its lilac centre deepened to a dark purple, and as she leaned forward, her face and shoulders were completely covered in the soft pulsating colour. Her head was spinning and a strange humming filled her ears. She blinked as the lavender-coloured mist cleared to reveal what looked like words that came and went, rippling in little waves. She screwed up her eyes as they floated into focus. It was some sort of message, written in spiky black writing:

Go to the painting that stands in the hall;
Let the story untold be the teller of all.

She watched as the letters began to shimmer then dance around each other before spiralling away like water down a plug-hole.

The next thing that Kirsty knew she was lying face down on the floor, the carpet rough against her cheek. Her gaze moved to the dressing-table. She crawled towards it, her heart fluttering in her chest as she looked in each of the open drawers. They were all empty. She reached a shaking hand inside the bottom one and rapped her knuckles against the hardwood base. It felt and sounded solid enough, with no sign of the purple pool or the strange message.

Shaking her head in disbelief, she clambered to her feet and staggered out of the room.

"*Ssslurp. Ssslurp.*"

Kirsty stuffed her knuckles into her mouth to stifle her screams at the sight of the thing that was crouched over the milky puddle of her spilt drink. It looked just like one of the long-snouted creatures that had been in the dressing-table. Its back was covered in shiny black hair and its tail was thin and pointed. Mean little red eyes darted furtively from side to side as it lapped up the milk. Flattening her body against the wall, she began to creep past the feeding beast. Her body was soaked with sweat as she made her way back along the corridor, only stopping once to check if Flora was still asleep.

Kirsty looked over her shoulder as she came to the top of the stairs. The creature was still there. It lifted its head to look at her, a white milk-moustache ringing its lips. It opened its mouth wide and she wasn't sure if it was just her imagination, but she was certain that she heard it laugh. It closed its long yellow teeth around the jam sandwich before disappearing down the passageway and into the night.

Shaking with fear, Kirsty gripped the banister and peered into the darkness. The black and white diamond-shaped tiles on the ground floor seemed to glow under the moonlight that filtered in through the tall windows. She padded down the stairs, holding her breath as each step creaked under her weight.

Kirsty shivered as her feet touched the cold floor. She looked nervously in the direction of the shadowy picture gallery. And then, with her heart pounding, she walked towards the stone archway and climbed the three steps.

Kirsty flicked on the light switch and stared at the huge oil painting of Bennachie, before turning slowly and mechanically towards the childhood portrait of her Mum, Aunt Flora and their little sister Elvira. She watched, fascinated, as a ball of light with a pulsating purple centre began to glow inside Elvira's chest.

The humming noise began again. Kirsty sniffed the air: the smell of flowers was back too. She looked on in amazement as the glowing globe separated itself from Elvira's body and moved towards her. It wove in and out between her bare feet and then circled her head before stopping right in front of her face. It burned brighter and brighter until it looked as if it was about to explode. She opened her mouth to scream.

Plop. Kirsty swallowed as the light-ball jumped onto her tongue then dropped to the bottom of her stomach. It felt as cold as ice and as she looked down she could see it through her dressing-gown, pulsing and dancing inside her. Then slowly, it began to move from her stomach to cover her heart.

Kirsty stretched her arms across the picture and flattened her body against it. She gasped as she felt her feet leave the floor. An invisible force was pulling her into the painting.

Chapter Six

Flanganans and the Book of Bennachie

Kirsty blinked as her eyes adjusted to bright sunlight. Her head moved from side to side as she looked down on Benderrie Manor, with its strange statues on one side and its standing stones on the other. Spreading her arms out wide, she floated down through the bluest sky that she had ever seen.

She gave a little squeal as she landed in the middle of the stone circle. The sound of laughter made her turn around. The three small sisters in the painting were right behind her.

"This can't be real." Kirsty rubbed her eyes. "I'm actually inside the picture." She could hear a bumble-bee humming and feel the warmth from the sun on her face. Reaching down, she picked a fluffy dandelion clock from the grass and blew into it, watching as the seeds floated away from her. She stretched out her legs and felt the tickle of grass behind her knees.

Kirsty turned towards the girls; they looked as if they'd been running and were red-faced and gasping for breath. Flora and Harriet were lying on their stomachs and Elvira was sitting with her back against a tree, a big book clasped against her heaving chest.

"Hello…" Kirsty crawled towards them. "Hello!" she shouted, sitting down cross-legged on the grass. "Can you hear me?"

The girls stared straight through her.

"Can you see me, Mum?" Kirsty blew into Harriet MacAlister's face. She didn't move or even blink. Then she plucked a buttercup from the grass and twirled it under her Aunt Flora's chin. The yellow shadow that the flower cast convinced her that this wasn't just another weird dream. It was real. She dropped the buttercup, watching as it twirled towards the ground like a tiny helicopter before coming to rest on top of the big brown book that Elvira held on her lap.

"Elvira!" Kirsty grabbed hold of the little girl's arm. She gasped as they touched: she had half-expected her fingers to pass right through her like in a ghost story that she'd seen on TV. But Elvira's flesh was warm and solid. She was real.

"I'm nae so sure that we should be doin' this." Flora was the first to speak. "I dinna think we should open it," she said, pulling the key from the lock on the book's cover and turning it around between her thumb and forefinger. "But then again…" she added, her eyes sparkling with excitement.

"NO!" shouted Harriet, putting her hand over the key-hole.

"Coward!" Elvira held the book up above her head. "Let's jist do it!"

"It's stealin'," said Harriet, giving Elvira a challenging stare. "An' you shouldn't take somethin' that isn't yours to take."

"Aye, she's right," interrupted Flora, changing her mind again. "An' if all those things you told us about what goes on doon there are true," she said, poking a fat finger into the grass, "then it belongs to them - the *Flumphaderries*."

"Well *they're* not here, are they?" Elvira blinked her odd eyes and grinned as she pointed towards the ground. "They're doon there."

"Go on then!" The silver key shone from Flora's plump palm. "I dare ye."

Elvira shot out a hand and grabbed it.

Kirsty chewed anxiously on her bottom lip as she watched the girls huddle over the book.

"No! Dinna." Harriet looked terrified and was nibbling nervously on her fingernails.

"Shut up!" shouted Elvira and Flora.

Kirsty held her breath as Elvira slid the key into the lock. It turned, clicked once and then stuck halfway round. A shower of sparks exploded into the air.

"Stop!" screamed Harriet.

But it was too late. The girls' eyes were wide with fear as a purple-coloured face appeared on the cover of the book, glowing with an eerie light.

Kirsty moved closer. The eyes on the book twitched twice before snapping open. They were pink and stared straight ahead. The slits of the narrow nostrils flared and the lips on the mouth stretched wide then slowly formed a big 'O'. A beautiful smell of flowers and a beam of lilac light streamed from the mouth as it began to speak:

"Within these pages lie all that is bad,
Evil kept prisoner,
'Neath Haroberd's hand.
Turn the key full circle,
And there's no going back -
Unleashing all that's wicked and black."

The lavender light disappeared and the face relaxed, the eyes closing as if in sleep.

"I'm scared. I think we should get rid of the book." Harriet looked terrified. "Give it to me. I'll throw it doon the well."

"Nae chance!" shouted Flora, punching her older sister on the shoulder. "There's no way we're givin' it back."

"Let's get it open before we change oor minds." Elvira seized the key and turned it the rest of the way.

"See, I told ye." She laughed as Harriet lunged at the book and pulled the key from the lock. "There's nothin' bad about it. It's only a stupid old book."

Kirsty watched as the key left Harriet's hand and somersaulted over and over in the air. She held her breath when she saw Elvira's arm reach out, her fingers closing around it as it landed in her upturned palm. All three girls crawled closer to the book. They sat on their knees and peered down at the sleeping face.

"Haaaaaaaaaa! Haaaaaaaaaa! Haaaaaaaaaa!"

A terrible sound ripped through the air. Green, foul-smelling smoke closed in around Kirsty. She gasped as thunder rumbled and a jagged zigzag of lightning split the summer sky.

She joined in with the sisters' screams as the book suddenly burst open. There was a smell like dog-dirt and a thing like a big black jelly blubbered up from the mouth on the cover. The revolting creature grew and grew until it was the size of a house. It turned and stared at them with its red eyes before turning and lumbering along the road that led back down into the village. Its feet made loud sucking noises and folds of slack skin scraped against the ground.

Kirsty watched as the monster slithered away in the direction of Bennachie, becoming smaller and smaller until it was just a little black speck.

A tortured groan and the sound of a distant splash made the sisters turn and look at each other.

"Maybe it's got as far as Bennachie an' gone doon Hosie's Well," said Elvira.

"Are ye crazy?" Harriet thumped her sister on the leg. "Didn't ye see the size of that...that thing? If it went doon the well it must have shrunk."

The girls screamed again as a loud bang and a cloud of sludge-coloured smoke cleared to show another terrible apparition crouched in front of them.

"GOT IT IN ONE, KID! That was Vasveegal, the big boss-man. He's an underground kinda guy. Vasveegal and daylight don't get on," the ugly looking beast sniggered, "the more he sees of it, the smaller he gets."

The creature wore green velvet shorts, a shiny red-and-yellow striped waistcoat and it spoke in a peculiar half-English, half-American accent. Its body was covered in long black hair, and as it stood up on its muscular hind legs, Kirsty could see that it was holding a gold fiddle in its leathery hands. It looked at them through the narrow slits of its red eyes. It opened its mouth; she could smell its vile breath and see the sticky strings of black gunge that stretched between its pointy teeth.

"Hi-YAAAAAA!" The beast danced around on the grass, trampling the buttercups with its clawed feet. It had a tail like a lion's that swished around its ankles.

"I wonder what else is inside this thing?" cried Elvira, picking up the book and sitting down on top of it.

"I'M OUT! Dickety-doo-daa! I'm out! I'm out!" The creature danced faster and faster, whirling around so quickly that Kirsty thought that it might drill a hole in the ground.

She held her breath as the smallest of the sisters pointed a shaking finger at the monster.

"Who are you?" asked Elvira, in a voice that was barely a whisper.

"Why, I'm Gananzzer of course." He threw back his head and laughed. "I'm the king of corruption. The sovereign of sin. The monarch of malevolence. The emperor of impudence." He pulled a bow from beneath his arm and tucked the golden fiddle under his chin. "I'm the wizard of wickedness," he added, as he began to play, his yellow claws moving like lightning over the strings.

Kirsty covered her ears with her hands to block out the terrible high-pitched screech of the violin.

Suddenly, the music stopped and the thing that called itself 'Gananzzer' tucked his golden instrument under one arm and hopped a little nearer to Elvira. "Give me the key, kid!" He stuck a wizened hand in front of her face and grinned, showing all his teeth.

Elvira shook her head. "Get lost!" she shouted, stuffing the key in her mouth. "Come any closer and I'll swallow it. I promise you…I will."

"I'll say this for you, you've got guts." Gananzzer picked up his tail and chewed on its black-haired tip. "And I kinda admire that in a kid. Mind you," his yellow teeth dropped down over his bottom lip as he sniggered, "I don't think that you're gonna be quite so cocky when you realise the kind of mess you're in."

"What do ye mean?" Elvira used her tongue to tuck the key into her cheek.

"*Elvira! Elvira! Say your name double*." He sang and laughed as he danced a wild jig. "*You've turned the key and now you're in trouble.*"

"Look, we dinna want anythin' to do with you or this lot." She nodded towards the book. "Jist disappear will ye?"

"Sorry." Gananzzer shook his head and made a clucking sound with his tongue. "No can do."

"I'm scared," whispered Harriet.

"Aw! My heart's bleeding, kiddo." He spun around to face her. "But your sister here should've thought of that before she opened the book - actions and consequences and all that jazz."

Gananzzer sat down cross-legged on the grass and twirled the long hair on his chin between his fingers. His tongue flicked over his black lips and his body swayed as he began to sing:

"Now that we're free, we've got work to do -
A kingdom to build - and it's all thanks to you!"

"What do you mean *we?*" asked Flora.

"Why don't you ask *her?*" Gananzzer pointed a crooked finger at Elvira. "Surely she's told you about the Flanganans?"

"We...we thought she was makin' it all up." Flora's voice wobbled as she spoke.

"Nope! It's all true. And we're every bit as bad as you were told. In fact," he threw back his long head and screamed with laughter, "WE'RE WORSE!"

Harriet and Flora began to cry and huddled closer to Elvira.

"Okay! Okay, about the Book of Bennachie." Gananzzer laid his head on one side and looked at the girls. "Its rules state that whoever opens it must accept full responsibility for what they've done, and then either Vasveegal or my good self is supposed to name them as the official Earth-bound Guardian of the Book and Key."

"Choose someone else!" cried Elvira. "I dinna want to be named."

"Tough luck, kiddo! Looks like you're stuck with the job. According to the rules, you're only allowed to share or pass on the responsibilities and powers of Guardian to your first-born child. But as you're only a kid yourself," sneered Gananzzer, "it doesn't look like you've got a whole lotta choice."

"Stop!" Elvira held up her hands.

"Okay. Okay. I can see that you're desperate, and rules are made to be broken. And as it doesn't exactly say *when* the Guardian has to be named - I guess we could put it off for a while...or, if you're really lucky - maybe forever."

"Forever sounds good," said Elvira.

"Okay dokey. Cos I kinda like you, here's what I'm gonna do." Gananzzer clapped his hairy hands together and grinned. "If you just give me the book and the key right now, we'll say no more about this Guardianship garbage. I'll take them both off your hands for good. This instant. Today. Eh? Eh? Whaddayasay?"

"Elvira! Get aff that book," screamed Harriet.

"Spit oot the key an' give it to him." Flora thumped a fist against her back.

"No!" Elvira began to back away. "I *want* to get rid of both of them, but I canna trust him."

Gananzzer looked furious, his shoulders shaking with rage. "I've gotta warn you," he said, strings of saliva beginning to stream from his bottom lip, "if you were stupid enough to try to turn the key again - well, I wouldn't even like to imagine what could happen to you."

"I winna! I promise!" wailed Elvira. "Jist…jist shove off an' leave us alone."

"Okay! Okay. I can see that your mind's made up." He wiped his mouth on the back of his hand. "But I have to say, you've put me in a kinda difficult position. If you won't hand over the goods, I'll have no other choice than to name you as the official Guardian."

"But I dinna want to be - "

"You're boring me now." Gananzzer crossed his arms. "I mean, wazza guy to do?" He sighed and scratched his head before adding, "But I wanna be fair. After all, if it wasn't for you I'd still be trapped. So…I'm gonna give you just one more chance to do as I ask." He pushed his face into hers and stared into her odd eyes. "So howzabout it? Eh?"

Elvira bit her lip and shook her head.

"Arrgh!" Gananzzer screamed and stamped with temper. "Okay kid, I've officially lost patience with you. The time for talking just ran out." He raised both arms in the air and began to chant:

> *"Here in the shadow of Bennachie -*
> *I name the Guardian of book and key.*
> *Elvi - "*

"STOP!" Elvira almost choked on the key. "I didna say that I wanted to keep them forever. Why don't you come later - when I've had time to think about it."

"Why should I?" Gananzzer put his hands on his hairy hips. "You can't have it both ways, kiddo. If you're not willing to give up the goods, and you won't accept the Guardianship either - then I'm afraid that means you're in my debt." He took a giant leap and landed right in front of her. "You owe me, kid. And it's my turn to call the shots. From now on, we're doing things on my terms." He laid his head on one side and gave her a sly smile.

"ANYTHING!" wailed Elvira. "Anything."

"Well now, let me see." Gananzzer drummed his twisted fingers against his chin. "Let's have some fun with this." His red eyes flickered as he pulled his golden fiddle from beneath his arm and began to pluck at its strings. "Let's make a deal." Green sparks flew from his yellow claws as he began to sing:

"*I'm in no hurry -*
It's not my style.
Hang on to the book -
At least for a while.
Enjoy your life, but don't forget,
A deal's a deal and a debt's a debt.
Let's make a plan for a rendezvous -
Many years from now, I'll wait for you.
I'll relieve you of the book and key,
And in exchange, you'll give to me:
Something made from flesh and bone;
A firstborn baby of your own,
A precious one, so sweet, so rare,
The child of the one with the odd-eyed stare."

"That sounds like a rhyme from some stupid, old-fashioned fairy story." Elvira covered her face with her hands and began to sob. "Jist go away. Leave us alone!"

"This ain't no fairy story, kiddo." Gananzzer's top lip peeled back in a sneering grin. "It's as real as real can be. And remember, if you don't hand over the book and the key when I come back for them, then I'm afraid that I'll have no other choice than to name you as official Guardian. Right there. On the spot." He showered her with sticky spit as he added, "But before you can get rid of me today, I need you to agree to the terms of my little contract."

"Okay!" shouted Elvira. "Now get lost!"

"Deal! Deal!" Gananzzer whooped with joy and did a little victory dance. "It's a dickety-doo-daa deal!"

Elvira leaned back on her heels as the book began to rock and vibrate under her. She screamed as it threw her off balance and floated up into the air. Using all her strength, she pushed it back down towards the grass. The face imprinted on the cover looked panic-stricken, its mouth opening and closing in a silent scream. The sky grew dark and a cold wind began to blow, flipping open the book and turning the pages.

"SEE YA, SUCKERS!" Gananzzer laughed and laughed, great ropes of saliva spewing from his open mouth and spinning around his head.

Kirsty covered her ears as the purple face began to scream.

The three sisters were thrown back against the grass as the book fell open at the centre pages and hundreds of black, rat-like creatures streamed out.

"FLANGANANS!" The girls looked desperately at each other.

"Follow me my little ones!" Gananzzer picked up his golden fiddle and played a wild tune on it as he skipped off down the road. He looked over a shaggy shoulder and winked at Elvira. "See ya on payback day!"

Kirsty watched as Elvira grabbed the book and the sisters began to run. She fell as she stood up to follow them, tumbling head over heels into the darkness, the sound of her own screams filling her head.

Chapter Seven

The Channelling Stone

Where am I now? wondered Kirsty, staring up into the starry darkness above her. Her hands moved over the weight that was pressing down on her chest and when she raised her head she saw that it was the book from the painting. She shivered as a thick mist crept up from the grass, covering her like a damp cloak.

Kirsty sat up and looked down at the book. She ran a hand over its cover. The face was asleep and the lock was empty. Trembling, she opened it.

The pages were stained a horrible yellowish-brown and the strange-looking writing inside the front leaf was black and spidery. Her lips moved as she began to read:

Praise Earth and bow to nature's might;
To plants and trees and birds of flight.
Praise moon and stars and sun on high,
The ground, the grass, the winds that sigh.
Respect this place and all things in it;
Eternal, breathing, living spirit.

Kirsty stared down at all the weird symbols, poems and beautiful pictures. She turned page after page until she came to the middle of the book: the centre sheets were stuck firmly together, a black gooey gunk oozing from around their tattered edges.

She screamed as an icy wind blew her hair back from her face and a terrible smell rose into the air.

RRRRIP. Kirsty watched in horror as the pages tore apart, the smelly glue dripping onto her hand. "Yuk!" she cried, wiping her fingers on the grass. "It's just like the stuff that sprayed out of the mouths of those beasts in the dressing-table."

Kirsty's eyes widened: empty black silhouettes of rat-like creatures filled every space on the paper. She traced their outlines before poking her fingers through the holes. A shiver shuddered up her spine as she thought of all the dark shapes that had escaped from the book and the horrible beast that she'd seen hunched over the spilt milk.

"*Kirsteeee.*" The eerie voice that Kirsty had heard before came back to haunt her. She stood up and pulled her dressing-gown tightly around her body, her bare feet sinking into the wet grass. She shrieked as the book began to shimmer and shake before finally breaking up and disappearing.

"This is all a dream." Her voice quivered as she brought her empty hands up to her face. "None of this is real, it's only my imagination."

As the mist suddenly cleared, Kirsty saw that she was standing in the middle of the stone circle. The huge grey slabs rose up from the ground, some straight, and others leaning in towards each other as if whispering a secret. Benderrie Manor sat against the night sky, its windows black and lifeless.

"Ugh!" She held her breath as something brushed against her bare legs. Goosebumps covered her skin as she slowly lowered her eyes.

Kirsty almost fainted with relief when she saw Hosie standing by her side. He purred and blinked his pink eyes as a little purple-centred circle of colour began to shine through his fur. She clutched her chest as a burning sensation began to radiate through her own body. And when she looked down, she saw that the ball of light that she had swallowed earlier was glowing again. Hosie cocked his head on one side and looked as if he was about to say something. And then he did.

"Come with me, Kirsty." He started to run. "Quickly!"

Kirsty followed Hosie, mud squelching between her bare toes. He stopped suddenly in front of one of the biggest stones. He stared straight ahead, his tail sticking out behind him.

"What is it?" gasped Kirsty, as she caught up with him.

"*This* is the Channelling Stone of Bennachie." Hosie waved a curled paw in the direction of the grey giant.

Kirsty shivered as its big black shadow fell across her face. She watched as Hosie padded closer to the stone. His ears pricked up as if listening intently, and then his body curved in the air as he began to levitate. Hosie melted into the darkness until only his head was still visible. He flicked a pink tongue over his lips and opened his mouth to speak:

"Channel the power from another world,
Here to this place called Bennachie.
Let Haroberd's light shine clear and bright,
True Guardian of the book and key."

Kirsty took a step back as the stone began to glow, glimmering and gleaming until it was just a solid block of purple light. The humming noise that she'd heard before buzzed around inside her head and a beautiful smell like a hundred flower gardens filled the air.

The ground under Kirsty's feet started to shake. And then suddenly, there before her stood two little figures.

She watched as one of them came towards her and raised both of its three-fingered hands in the air. It gazed deep into her eyes. And then it nodded and looked as if it had found the answer to a question.

Kirsty tripped over a boulder as she backed away. She raised herself up on her elbows and stared at the strange life-form.

She shook her head, thinking, *you're like nothing I've ever seen before: like something from another planet.*

"I am," said the creature. "I'm from the planet Derrius."

Her jaw dropped. "You read my mind?" she croaked.

"Correct again." It blinked and smiled.

Kirsty felt as if she was dreaming as she gawped at the two bizarre beings: they were a pale violet colour and had big pink eyes and flat noses with a square patch of red skin which wrinkled when they spoke. They wore tiny togas made from a weave of heather and glossy green leaves. A purple heart was glowing and beating slowly inside their chests and the uncovered parts of their bodies looked soft and transparent, rows of little pink bubbles travelling tirelessly under their skins in an endless circuit. Their webbed feet made no sound as they shuffled around on the wet grass, a blue brain throbbing inside each perfectly rounded, hairless head.

"Hosie! Where are you?" Kirsty suddenly remembered about Aunt Flora's cat.

"I'm here!" said the other small alien.

"Hosie?" She moved a little closer. "Is that you?"

"I'm a Derrian too," he looked at his friend, "we both are."

"Derrian? Derrius? I don't have a clue what you're talking about." Kirsty covered her face with her hands and began to sob.

"Don't be afraid. We won't hurt you." He reached out and stroked her hair. "But we *do* need your help."

"I don't want to help you," said Kirsty, wiping her tear-stained face on the sleeve of her dressing-gown.

"Let me introduce myself." The first extraterrestrial's wide mouth stretched into a toothless smile. "I am Nacnud," he turned and pointed to his companion, "and his name is Leardrim."

"This isn't really happening." Kirsty shook her head.

Nacnud closed his eyes for a moment before tilting his face towards the night sky. A single shaft of purple light sliced through the darkness and covered him in a wide circle of brightness.

"I want to go home," cried Kirsty.

"So do we." Leardrim sighed and grasped his friend's hand.

"What's wrong with him?" asked Kirsty, when she saw Nacnud's shoulders slump. Tears that sparkled like diamonds trickled down his cheeks. Her eyes widened in wonderment as the droplets became solid and bounced off her foot before disappearing into the wet grass.

"Haroberd is asking if we are ready to return to Derrius." Leardrim held a hand on either side of his head as if he was receiving some sort of message.

"Who's Haroberd?" Kirsty turned towards Nacnud. His face was full of sorrow and he looked as if his heart might break.

"Look up." Leardrim put an arm around her shoulders.

Kirsty raised her eyes: millions of stars glittered against the blackness. She shivered; although Leardrim's arm felt as if it was made of jelly, the pink bubbles that moved under his skin crunched and crackled when they touched.

"We come from a planet called Derrius," he explained, his eyes filling up with tears as he pointed towards the night sky. "We only intended to stay for a short time - but we've been stranded here for over twenty Earth years."

"What happened?" Kirsy stared at the full moon as if it might answer her question.

"Come!" He held out his hands. "And I will show you everything."

Kirsty followed Leardrim into the purple spotlight, the glowing globe that lay over her heart beginning to burn inside her chest. They all joined hands and made a circle. She gave a little squeal as her feet left the ground.

"Don't be afraid," said Leardrim. "We won't let anything happen to you."

Kirsty screamed as they suddenly shot up into the sky and hung in mid-air, the circle of stones beneath them bathed in moonlight. Vibrating fans of skin like miniature wings protruded from Nacnud and Leardrim's backs.

"You can fly?" Her head jerked from side to side as she looked around. To her right, she could see Benderrie Manor, and beyond, the yellow street lamps of Weerdee. And straight in front of her, against a mantle of stars, stood a black Bennachie.

"Hold on tightly." Nacnud gave her fingers a comforting squeeze.

"You'll be quite safe," assured Leardrim.

Kirsty gave a cry of panic as they began to fly through the air. The wind pushed her hair back from her face as they rose higher and higher before dropping down towards the heathery mountain slopes.

"Kick your legs out behind you." Leardrim tightened his grip.

"Keep your head down and hold your arms close to your body," instructed Nacnud. "And when I say *now*," he turned to look at her, his pink eyes huge and unblinking, "I want you to hold your breath."

"Stop!" yelled Kirsty, as grass and jagged boulders rushed up to meet them. "We're going to crash!"

"NOW!" shouted Nacnud.

Kirsty took a deep gulp of the cold night air as they stopped and hovered for a moment above the well her Aunt Flora had warned her to stay away from.

Her whole body shook as it hit the pool of ice-cold water.

Chapter Eight

The Flumphaderries

Kirsty screamed as Nacnud and Leardrim let go of her wrists and were carried away on a torrent of raging white water, their small bodies bouncing along as they disappeared from sight.

"Come back!" she gurgled. "Don't leave me!"

The winding waterway went on and on like some terrifying carnival ride, twisting and turning, faster and faster. Then suddenly, she was plunged into darkness and falling. Over and over she went, her arms spinning and her legs pedalling madly in mid-air as she dropped. Down. Down…

Kirsty's eyes were wide with fear as she plunged into a deep pool. Kicking her legs out behind her she fought her way to the surface, gasping for air as she pushed her hair back from her brow and looked around.

"Nacnud! Leardrim!" she shouted. "Where are you?"

Swoosh. Chunk.

Kirsty's mouth fell open as a block at the bottom of the stone wall slid upwards. A puff of pink smoke wheezed from the space.

A slight breeze ruffled her hair and made little ripples on the water. And then, much to her amazement, two furry-looking green balls rolled out and came towards her.

Kirsty took a deep breath and sank down deeper, treading water furiously, with only the top half of her face visible above the surface.

"Follow us." One of the balls rolled closer to the edge of the pool.

"Quickly!" urged the other. It sounded impatient and moved in little circles.

Kirsty swam to the side. She stretched out a hand and touched each of the green balls, then drew back in surprise: they were made of moss, soft and springy under her fingers.

The moss-balls didn't speak again. They began to vibrate before moving towards each other and then vanishing through the gap.

Kirsty pulled herself out of the water, her feet and hands slipping and sliding on the slimy sides of the pool. She crawled on her hands and knees and lay flat on her stomach in front of the place where the moss-balls had gone. Then, taking a big lungful of the damp-smelling air, she pushed her head and shoulders through the opening. She lay for a moment with her face pressed against the wet stone floor.

"*Come!*" said another voice, louder this time and more insistent.

Following the command, Kirsty wormed her way along a narrow corridor. She almost screamed out loud as a huge spider ran in front of her face and then straight into the jaws of a gigantic green toad.

GGRRRRGRIBBUGE. The toad made a disgusting sound like a giant burp. A long tongue flicked from its mouth and whipped itself around the spider's legs as it tried to scuttle away. She hardly dared to breathe as the chewing creature lumbered towards her. It came so close that she found herself staring straight into its watery, red-veined eyes. Then she did scream. She screamed long and loud, scraping her knuckles on the rocky floor as she pushed away the horrible wobbly body and scrambled towards the end of the corridor.

Kirsty cried with relief as the passageway finally opened out into a much wider space. She got to her feet and looked around: she was standing in a chamber with a large circular opening in its wall. She poked her head through the hole and saw that it was the entrance to another, much bigger tunnel.

"*Welcome*." The voice that she had heard earlier echoed from its depths.

Kirsty glanced behind her, remembering the toad and the spider; *she couldn't go back*.

Suddenly, a dazzling light began to shine. One of the moss-balls came hurtling towards her. It stopped halfway along the passage and then started to go back the way that it had come.

She jumped into the white-walled tunnel and ran. Faster and faster she went, her legs beginning to ache as the moss-ball gathered speed, rolling towards the brightness.

*

Kirsty stood in front of the light, watching as its lilac centre began to glow. And as she looked down, she saw her own purple heart beating inside her chest. She opened her arms wide and melted into its radiance.

Kirsty couldn't believe her eyes as she stepped out of the light and into a place that she was sure must be heaven. She gave a puzzled frown as she looked around - everything was bathed in sunshine, but there was no sun in the sky.

"It never gets dark here," said the moss-ball, reading her mind. "Darkness attracts evil."

"This place is so beautiful," she whispered, gazing at the fields of flowers. "I've never seen so many shades of the same colour."

"Purple, in its pure form and in its many shades," said the moss-ball at her feet, "is the colour of peace, love, healing and harmony." A slit appeared in the green ball and a pair of lilac webbed feet emerged, the toes wriggling in the warm sunlight. Seconds later, Leardrim clambered from the mossy disguise like a chick hatching from an egg. He stood in front of her, his blue brain pulsing inside the bald dome of his head.

Kirsty felt a shiver of excitement run through her body as he put his boneless hand in hers and led her into the amazing landscape.

She blinked in disbelief as Leardrim took her through fields of fragrant flowers and over gloriously green grass. Fountains of frothy white water flowed into streams that ran over rocks and under bridges.

"Come. We must get on." He tugged at her arm. "Haroberd is waiting."

"*Who* or *what* is Haroberd? And where are you taking me now?" Kirsty tried to pull away from Leardrim when she saw the tiny fans of skin re-emerge from his back. He linked his arm through hers and they began to fly, moving quickly and so close to the ground that she could smell the flowers.

She held her breath as they finally stopped above a glittering lake.

"Can you row?" Leardrim nodded towards a set of oars as their feet touched down on the deck of a glass boat.

"Take us out to the middle," he said, his wings folding and disappearing from sight.

Kirsty rowed until they reached the centre of the lake.

"Haroberd is ready." Leardrim bowed his head, his forehead furrowing in concentration.

Kirsty watched as a purple bubble began to rise from the bottom of the boat. It grew bigger and bigger, blowing up like a huge balloon. It wobbled and quivered as it stretched to cover first the boat and then the entire lake.

"*WELCOME.*" A loud voice made her jump.

"What's going on?" She lunged forward, the oars falling into the water.

Suddenly the roof of the giant bubble stopped moving. It changed to a bright white and looked solid.

"Lie on your back," said Leardrim, moving to the end of the glass vessel.

Kirsty did as she was told and felt as if she was looking up at a giant movie screen. Swirling colours and images began to form above her.

"*I AM HAROBERD, PROTECTOR AND LEADER OF THE DERRIANS.*"

She put her hands over her ears as the booming voice seemed to swell to fill the bubble. The spinning colours slowed down to reveal a face with thick lips and bright pink eyes.

"Don't be scared." Leardrim jumped into the water. His six fingers curled over the side of the boat as his gaze met hers. "The next thing you will see will be my home on the planet Derrius."

Kirsty watched as the film show began.

The roof of the bubble turned as black as night. Millions of white stars sparkled against the darkness, casting their light on a detailed diagram of the sun and the family of planets, asteroids and comets that orbit it. And then they all moved to one side and were replaced by a giant three-fingered hand that pointed to a place far beyond the Earth's solar system.

Kirsty nodded, tears tightening her throat as she understood what Haroberd was trying to show her. Leardrim and Nacnud really were aliens, creatures from another planet: another world.

Leardrim seemed to read her mind again and closed his little hand around hers as hundreds of images of a strange and wondrous place played on and on above them. Thousands of tiny creatures that looked just like Leardrim were living their lives in a place that she had never heard of.

"What are you doing on Bennachie, when you could live on Derrius?" She turned towards Leardrim and saw that he was close to tears.

"Good question." He picked up the oars and hauled himself back into the boat.

"Then tell me the answer," said Kirsty, as the images above her head began to fade away.

"It was Elvira's fault." Leardrim squeezed into the narrow seat and buried his head in his purple arms.

"How can you blame my Aunt Elvira?" asked Kirsty.

"I *don't* blame her." Leardrim looked up and stroked the back of her hand with one of his long fingers. "I…we loved her." He shrugged his shoulders and sighed before adding, "Truth is, though, it was Elvira who let them out."

Kirsty swallowed hard as an image of the black shapes that had escaped from the book flashed through her mind.

Leardrim's voice dropped to a whisper. "Haroberd rules that we can never return to Derrius until the evil that was unleashed on Bennachie is back under lock and key."

Kirsty shook her head in confusion.

"Let me explain." Leardrim shuffled his tiny bottom along the glass deck. He blinked his pink eyes, the patch of skin on his nose creasing as he began to speak:

"On Derrius we have developed in a way that humans can only dream of." His mouth curved upwards in a smile at the mention of his home. "We have no hate; only love. We have no greed; only selflessness - "

"So why leave?" asked Kirsty.

Leardrim held up a silencing hand. "We were attracted to Bennachie, not only because of its outstanding natural beauty, but because the spirit and magical power of nature is so strong here. It was our second visit and we only intended to stay for a short study trip..." he sighed then, his soft shoulders rounding over.

"Tell me more." Kirsty felt sorry for Leardrim when she saw the sadness in his eyes.

"Derrius wasn't always such a wonderful place," he continued. "Once, there was a dark side to our planet: a place of wickedness and evil, ruled by a malicious Master and his equally awful associate. The Master ruled over an army of lost souls and was ruthless in his quest for power."

"What's a lost soul?" asked Kirsty.

"One without a conscience," explained Leardrim. "When you can't tell the difference between right and wrong your soul is lost forever to the darkness."

"And this Master, where is he now?"

"Patience, my friend." He pressed a finger against her lips. "Haroberd found a way of containing the sinful souls. He transformed them into terrible-looking beasts and kept them imprisoned in a book of the '*Old Magic*', which I found on an ancient settlement on our first visit to Bennachie. They were frozen to the pages: seeing and hearing everything that went on outside the book, but unable to move or communicate." He sounded angry with himself and paused before adding, "Everything would have been fine if Elvira hadn't gone down Hosie's Well."

"What happened?" Kirsty could hardly wait to hear what he had to say.

"The book's care was entrusted to me." Leardrim looked embarrassed. "And what happened next was my mistake - I expected too much of the child. You see, I told her all about myself and Nacnud and our life on Derrius."

"What did she do?"

"Elvira promised not to tell anyone about us, but she stole Haroberd's book and took it up to the surface to share its secret with her sisters."

"I...I'm sorry," said Kirsty, feeling suddenly responsible for the actions of the three little girls.

"Hush." Leardrim seemed to understand how she was feeling and stretched one of his bendy arms around her shoulders. "Elvira decided that, as we came from the planet Derrius, she would call us 'Flumphaderries' and," he managed a little laugh, "she even named the evil creatures that were incarcerated in the book. She called them - "

"Flanganans," interrupted Kirsty. "That's why you took me inside the painting." She felt a wave of excitement surge through her body. "You wanted to show me what had happened."

"That's right." Leardrim nodded his bald head. "We want you to understand… because we need your help."

How can I help you? thought Kirsty. *I'm no one special.*

"That's just where you're wrong," said Leardrim, reading her mind. "I can't explain everything just yet, but I want you to know that you *are* very special - very special indeed."

"So where are they now - these Flanganans?" Kirsty had forgotten to be afraid of Leardrim and put both hands on his marshmallow shoulders.

"Start rowing!" he said. "And I'll show you."

When they reached the edge of the lake, Nacnud was waiting.

Leardrim smiled at his companion as he stepped ashore and shook himself dry.

"Be careful." Nacnud threw his moss-ball into Leardrim's arms.

"We'll be fine." Leardrim passed the disguise to Kirsty. "Put this on," he said, pulling his own furry green shell from his toga and stepping into it. "We're going up to the top!"

Chapter Nine

Payback Day

Kirsty clasped her hands around her legs and tucked her knees under her chin as she rolled along after Leardrim, moving so fast that she wondered if they were flying again. The inside of the moss-ball smelt of damp earth and was soft against her face as she peered through its narrow opening.

"This is as far as we go." Leardrim stopped outside an opening in a wall. "Follow me," he said, rolling inside and stepping out of his moss-ball.

Kirsty clambered out of her own disguise and watched as Leardrim placed his webbed feet on two slippery slabs of stone.

"Come on!" He crooked a finger in the air. "Jump up behind me."

Kirsty pushed her moss-ball into the pocket of her dressing-gown and climbed up to join him.

"Kneel down and put your arms around me." He turned and gave her a toothless smile. "And hold on tight!"

She screamed as Leardrim began to use his weight to rock the stones. Once. Twice. Three times.

Whoosh! A single shaft of light came hurtling towards them, blinding them both and lifting them into the air.

"Help!" Kirsty clasped her hands around Leardrim's chest and buried her face in his back.

When Kirsty lifted her head, she saw that they were floating inside what looked like a very dark and narrow lift shaft.

"We're trapped!" She felt dizzy and breathless as she pressed a hand against one of the cold walls.

"Don't panic," said Leardrim. "Trust me."

"Where are we?"

"We're inside the Channelling Stone. We go below earth through the right-hand side of Hosie's well, and return to the surface by the stone."

There was a bang and a purple flash and the next thing Kirsty knew she was back in the middle of the standing stones.

She shivered as she watched Leardrim stretch his small body. The fans of skin reappeared from his back; humming and spinning, they lifted him off his feet.

"It's dark, so I think we can manage without these." He stuffed his moss-ball inside his clothes and offered Kirsty his hand.

"Where are we going now?" she asked, almost recoiling when his skin crackled under her fingers.

"Just keep a tight hold," said Leardrim. "And remember how I told you to fly."

Kirsty's chest hurt as she took deep gulps of the cold night air. She kicked her legs out behind her as they flew, keeping her free arm tucked tightly into her side.

They rose high in the sky, leaving Benderrie Manor and the stone circle behind them. Kirsty looked down at the yellow street lamps of Weerdee; apart from a light that was shining from the school window, all the buildings were in darkness.

"Going down!" cried Leardrim, as they began their descent.

They flew along the line of the chimney tops, before dropping to the ground outside Weerdee Primary School.

"Stay close to the ground." Leardrim put a hand on Kirsty's back and pushed her down onto the grass verge.

She watched him shuffle towards the light that was shining from the assembly hall window. He pulled himself up onto the sill and peered through a gap in the curtains.

"What is it?" Kirsty crawled towards him, shivering as her bare knees touched the wet grass. "What can you see?"

"*Sshh.*" Leardrim's six fingers gripped the window ledge. His bald head bobbed back and forth and he seemed to be watching something.

Kirsty joined him, keeping as near to the ground as she could.

"They're all here," he said, little pink puffs of air escaping from his mouth, "planning their next move."

"There's Mrs Sookhard from the sweet shop," said Kirsty. "And Mrs Hardpiece from the tearoom with Mr Savage the butcher. Oh no!" She felt herself beginning to blush. "There's Miss Knowall, my new teacher."

"I'm almost certain," said Leardrim, turning to face her, "that these four horrible specimens are really Flanganans in disguise."

"But they're *real* people." Kirsty trembled with fear as she moved a little closer to Leardrim.

"They may look human," he said, giving a small twist of a smile, "but like me, Flanganans can transform into anything they wish. They can alter their appearance and even grow a second skin for a more permanent disguise. They also have the power to make places and people disappear."

"Look what they're doing," whispered Kirsty, pulling on Leardrim's arm. She watched as the shopkeepers and her headmistress moved back a few steps to reveal what looked like a giant black cooking pot with a small camping stove burning beneath it. Each of them took it in turns to go over to the pan and spit into it. And every time they spat, the great gobs of sticky black liquid fizzed and bubbled and a thin ribbon of green smoke rose into the air.

"Yuck! What is that stuff?" Kirsty shouted so loudly that Miss Knowall stopped what she was doing and turned towards the window.

"Sit down and shut up!" Leardrim yanked at the collar of her dressing-gown. "We need to talk."

"You're scaring me," said Kirsty, falling down onto the grass verge. The school wall felt cold and hard against her back as she leaned against it.

"I want to show you something." Leardrim closed his eyes and pressed one of his fingers against the small patch of wrinkly red skin on his nose.

Kirsty stared as the square of skin began to glow with a bright, white light. It started to grow wider, shining and stretching until it looked like a small computer screen.

"Come closer." Leardrim knelt in front of Kirsty. He held her face between his hands and brought her forehead down to rest against his own.

A tingling feeling ran through her body, and when she looked down she could see coloured lights and shapes moving quickly across Leardrim's nose.

"Do you remember the pact that Elvira made with Gananzzer?" He raised his eyes to look into hers.

"I…I think so," she said.

"Well, Elvira had almost forgotten Gananzzer's deal. In fact, she had begun to think that she had imagined the whole thing, when…"

"What?" Kirsty tried to pull away. "Tell me!"

"My memory display will show you what happened," said Leardrim. "I'll take you back in time eleven years. Watch and listen."

Kirsty stared as the coloured shapes and lights slowed down. The tiny screen flickered for a moment before making a loud hissing noise, then cleared to show a picture of a red-haired woman sitting in a rocking-chair. A man with a black moustache and even blacker hair gazed adoringly at the baby in the woman's arms. The infant had lots of dark hair and had a contented smile on its face. A black cat, which looked like Hosie, was perched on the back of the rocker.

"It's Elvira and Charlie," said Kirsty, remembering the wedding portrait that Flora had shown her. "And that must be you disguised as Hosie…and the baby must be Roanna." She sighed; a strange feeling of sadness which she couldn't explain brought hot tears to her eyes.

"Oh!" Her head began to feel fuzzy and strange. She covered Leardrim's hands with her own as her body swayed. Her forehead felt as if it was melting into his and then she screamed as all the colours disappeared and were replaced with a dazzling white glow.

When Kirsty's eyes adjusted to the light, she saw that she was floating in the air above Elvira, Charlie and their baby. The sweet smell of talcum powder and the sound of Hosie's purring filled the air. Her back scraped against the ceiling and when she looked down she could see that she was in the room that Flora had forbidden her to enter. Clean white nappies and two matching pink baby jackets hung over the end of a big wooden cot. And through the tall window stood Bennachie, bathed in sunlight and covered in a carpet of purple heather.

Kirsty held her breath as she began to drop down towards the rocker. Down...down she went, until she passed right through Elvira and found herself sitting on the chair's velvet cushion. She shook her head and gasped in disbelief as she looked around; she was inside Elvira's body and seeing everything through her eyes.

Kirsty could hear the muffled thump of Elvira's heart, the soft sound of her breathing and the gentle lullaby that she was humming to her baby. She tried to blink, but her eyes stayed wide open. She tried to stand up and move away, but found that she was stuck fast to the seat. And although she knew that she should have felt afraid, somehow she didn't: she felt warm and safe and...loved. Her gaze moved to the baby who lay cradled in Elvira's arms. Its eyes were big and blue and a damp curl lay against its tiny forehead.

Then suddenly, the atmosphere in the room changed. Hosie's tail began to sway from side to side and his fur stood up on end. His body arched as he hissed and spat and bared his teeth. The air became cold and the sky outside the window grew dark, big storm clouds gathering over Bennachie.

The sash window slid open and a hideous hairy face appeared on the sill. Kirsty screamed in horror - it was Gananzzer, the horrible beast that had escaped from the book.

"*Rock-a-bye-baby*," sang the creature, sniffing the air. "DO I SMELL A CHILD?"

Gananzzer wore a frilly yellow bonnet, the satin ribbons dangling down beneath his long snout. Two pointy teeth hung over his bottom lip and he was sucking furiously on a pink plastic dummy.

Kirsty heard Elvira's heart begin to beat faster, racing along beside her own.

"Remember me, EL.VI.RA?" The beast sounded each syllable of her name then shrieked with laughter, saliva springing from his mouth as he spat the dummy onto the floor.

"What do ye want?" Elvira picked up her baby and held her close.

Kirsty tried to put her arms around Roanna too, but found that she was powerless to protect her.

"Well, I think we both *know* what I want. Don't we?" Gananzzer's red eyes darted around the room before coming to rest on Roanna.

"Well, ye canna have her," said Elvira. "Ye see, I...I've changed my mind. I dinna need ye to take the book or the key anymore. I've decided to keep them both... forever."

"But it's payback day and you can't just go rewriting the terms of our little contract. If I remember rightly, I didn't name you as Guardian outta the goodness of my heart. And then, I agreed to take the book and the key off your hands at a later date in return for a child of your own. Correctamundo?"

"That's what I said then, but - "

"But nothin', kid. That's what we agreed and that's the way it's gonna stay. GOT IT?" Gananzzer wiped his hands on his red and yellow waistcoat then rested his head on his muscular forearms. He grinned, showing all his teeth. "It's like I told you before: a deal's a deal and a debt's a debt."

Kirsty felt a huge wave of sympathy for Elvira and Charlie wash over her when she saw the look of panic that passed between them.

"OKAY! Okay." Gananzzer examined his long yellow fingernails. "You obviously need a little time to reconsider. So..." He gave a cruel snigger. "Howzabout you meet me at Hosie's Well at sunrise tomorrow, with the book, the key and the kid?"

Kirsty could hear Elvira sobbing softly.

"Then it's a deal." There was a dull thud as Gananzzer dropped from the windowsill. "It's a dickety-doo-daa-deal!"

Kirsty screamed as an invisible hand seemed to pull her from Elvira's body. And then she was back on the grass verge with her forehead pressed against Leardrim's.

Chapter Ten

Gananzzer's Revenge

"That was horrible." Kirsty rubbed her eyes and shook her head.

"Not nearly as bad as what happened next," said Leardrim, pulling himself up to look through the assembly hall window.

"They're still busy," he said, dropping back down onto the grass, "so I should have time to finish my story."

Kirsty wrapped her dressing-gown tightly around her as the dampness from the grass crept up through her body.

"Elvira and Charlie were sick with worry, they just didn't know what to do for the best. Elvira still didn't want to be named as Guardian, but she knew that she could never part with her own flesh and blood. She was also afraid of what Gananzzer might do if he had the book and key in his possession."

He took a deep breath before continuing: "But by that evening they had thought of a plan. Elvira and Harriet persuaded Flora to use her exceptional artistic talents to make a replica book. She covered it in cracked brown leather from an old chair and stained the pages with tea to make them look ancient. It was an almost perfect copy and when she'd finished they were all satisfied that Gananzzer wouldn't be able to tell that it wasn't the real Book of Bennachie."

"But what about the key?" asked Kirsty.

"Elvira used the key and the lock from her jewellery box and fitted it onto the cover of the new book."

"And then she took it to -"

"Hosie's Well, with Charlie and baby Roanna," interrupted Leardrim. "Harriet stayed at home to guard the real book and key and your Aunt Flora and I followed on Scarlet."

"What happened next?" asked Kirsty, eager to hear the rest of the tale.

"Well, sunrise came and so did Gananzzer." Leardrim looked sad, a string of jewelled tears dropping from the end of his chin and disappearing into the long grass. "He shot out from behind a boulder in a blaze of blue and yellow flames. Sparks were flying from his claws as he leapt around on the heather, dancing to a tune on his golden fiddle."

"And did he take the book and the baby?"

"Neither," said Leardrim. "Elvira and Charlie had never any intention of handing over their child; they'd planned to make a run for it just as soon as Gananzzer had the replica book in his hands."

"But you said he didn't take it either?"

"He didn't. He noticed immediately that it was a copy and he was furious. He ranted and raved and then he amazed Elvira by telling her that she could keep her baby *and* get out of being named as official Guardian, if she handed over the real book and the key right away."

"So he didn't really want Roanna and he never had any intention of naming Elvira either." Kirsty felt breathless with excitement. "All that he wanted was to have the book for himself."

"That's right," said Leardrim. "And the reason that he didn't name Elvira on the day that she opened it was to stop her having power over him - you see, turning the key back around is the only way that the Guardian can recapture the Flanganans."

"But he was still afraid that she might be able to," said Kirsty, suddenly understanding everything. "That's why he warned her never to try to turn the key, it was for his protection, not hers."

"Top marks! Exactly right." Leardrim stood up to check that the shopkeepers were still inside the assembly hall before carrying on with his story:

"Gananzzer flew into a wild rage when Elvira and Charlie took to their heels and ran down Bennachie. He ripped the pages from the book and threw it into the air and then Hosie - I mean *I*, jumped onto your Aunt Flora's back and we escaped on Scarlet."

"Then what happened?" Kirsty moved closer to Leardrim, enthralled by the tale.

"Flora had stopped Scarlet in the middle of the stone circle and we were watching from behind the Channelling Stone." Leardrim covered his face with his hands and his blue brain seemed to tremble inside his head. "Gananzzer screamed with fury and chased after Elvira, Charlie and Roanna. They ran and ran, but not fast enough to escape him. They'd almost reached Benderrie Manor when he caught up with them in the woods across from where we were hiding. Three giant steps and he was upon them. He opened his mouth and covered them in a stream of sticky slime and then, as they struggled to free themselves, he turned them all to stone."

"The statues in the wood on the road to the Manor." Kirsty covered her mouth with her hands. "That's them! Isn't it?"

Leardrim nodded. "Gananzzer was furious. He stamped his feet with rage and screeched, 'I'll teach you to make a fool of me!' Then he pointed his gnarled finger, first at Elvira and then at Roanna and shouted:

'I'll set you in stone for all to see,
And name two Guardians of the book and key.
Elvira and her first-born baby there -
Child of the one with the odd-eyed stare.'

"And then Gananzzer screamed with laughter and added:

'Turn the key back around to set yourselves free,
Recapture the evil and save Bennachie.'"

"But that's not fair," said Kirsty. "If Elvira *and* Roanna have both been turned to stone, how *can* they turn the key?"

Leardrim looked like he was about to say something, then closed his mouth and shook his head.

"And what about the real book," said Kirsty. "Where is it now?"

"Flora wears the key on a chain around her neck and the book is in its hiding place," he lowered his voice to a whisper, "in a secret compartment under the seat of the rocking-chair. That's why your Aunt Flora doesn't go into Elvira and Charlie's bedroom: when she put the book back after Gananzzer's visit, the chair began to glow in the dark and rock on its own."

Kirsty nodded, remembering the wooden blocks that were wedged under the chair's runners. "Is the room... haunted?"

"Not haunted exactly." Leardrim gave a nervous smile. "But plenty of strange things have happened in there since that fateful day: voices, mysterious lights and noises. It's a constant battle between good and evil." He sighed. "Up until now righteousness has always won...but for how much longer?"

"I know that you're not the official Guardians," said Kirsty, "but if you know where the book is hidden, why haven't you or Nacnud tried to turn the key back around yourselves? If you want to go home to Derrius, it's got to be worth a try."

"I'm afraid it's not quite that simple. We've been waiting for a long time for all the Flanganans to come above ground." Leardrim took a deep breath. "We have to make sure that every last one of them is in the same place before we can try to recapture them." He lowered his voice and added, "And that means Vasveegal and Gananzzer too."

"Well, I don't want to have anything to do with it," said Kirsty anxiously.

"But you've got to help us, Kirsty. We need you - *Weerdee* needs you. I can't explain everything right now." He smiled and touched her cheek. "But I'm asking you to trust me. I'm certain that the Flanganans are going to try to take over the village at tomorrow's Fair. I'm not sure exactly what they're planning; I just know that it will be something terrible." His purple brow pleated with concern. "And if we don't stop them - "

"First Weerdee - and then the world." Kirsty's voice rose as she began to panic.

"*Ssshh.*" Leardrim put a hand over her mouth as a noise came from the assembly hall. They both jumped to their feet, then crouched down outside the window.

Miss Knowall and the shopkeepers were screaming with laughter as they took turns to stir the contents of the cooking pot with a massive wooden spoon. Grinning, they passed the spoon around, their curly pink tongues licking at the sticky-looking strings of black goo. They all nodded and smiled with approval as they poured the liquid into a huge baking tray.

Kirsty felt every muscle in her body tense as Miss Knowall and her friends suddenly stopped and turned towards the window. They raised their heads and seemed to sniff the air.

"Oh no!" whispered Leardrim. "They must have smelt us. A Flanganan's eyesight is poor but its sense of smell is exceptional."

Kirsty stared as the fearsome four began to claw and pull at their faces: under each human disguise was the most disgusting and frightening-looking creature that she had ever seen. Loose skin hung around their necks like Halloween masks as they began to march towards the door.

"Run!" Leardrim grabbed Kirsty's arm and pulled her along the street.

They sprinted around to the side of Mrs Sookhard's sweet shop. Leardrim jumped up on Kirsty's shoulders and rattled one of the old windowpanes. "Come on! We've got to hide," he said. A shower of cracked white paint fell to the ground as he forced it open and scrambled inside.

"Help me!" cried Kirsty. "I can hear them coming." She pulled herself up onto the sill and Leardrim seized her wrists, lifting her up and through the window.

She dropped down to a narrow shelf full of rattling Irn Bru bottles.

"Come on," urged Leardrim, leaping onto Mrs Sookhard's long serving counter. "Jump!"

Kirsty took a deep breath and followed him, her heart missing a beat as she slipped on the polished wood and knocked the brass scales onto the floor. The loud clanging noise filled the shop.

"Quiet!" Leardrim caught hold of her leg and pulled her down beside him. They sat together on the bare wooden boards, their knees pulled up to their chins. Moonlight streamed through the shop's front window, illuminating the menacing black shadows that lurked in every corner.

"*Silly little Miss Imagination…*" Kirsty's voice shook as she began to recite one of the little rhymes that always made her feel better when she was scared.

"Hush! I can hear someone." Leardrim held up a hand.

Kirsty felt her whole body tremble when the sound of footsteps on gravel stopped outside the shop. Her heart was bumping against her ribs and her face and hands were soaked in sweat.

"Kirsty! Are you in there?"

Kirsty leapt to her feet and peered over the edge of the counter.

She felt her whole body sag with relief when she saw Brodie clambering through the window. Jane was holding on to the leg of his pyjamas and he knocked a glass bottle off the shelf as he turned to help her.

"Hurry up you two! Get in." Kirsty watched as the bottle rolled across the floor, orange fizz escaping from its lid as it hit the edge of the counter.

"What are you two doing here?" asked Kirsty, helping Brodie and Jane climb down. "Why aren't you in bed?"

"I was." Brodie yawned so widely that it looked like he might swallow his own head. "I got up for somethin' to eat," he said sleepily, his brace glinting in the moonlight, "an' that's when I saw you an' this weird lookin' kid runnin' across the street."

"He knocked on my bedroom window an' woke me up," said Jane, shivering in her thin pink nightie. "We followed ye." Her black hair seemed to disappear into the darkness and her white face looked like a mask.

"So where's yer pal?" asked Brodie.

"I…I don't know." Kirsty looked around. "Leardrim! Where are you? It's okay. Brodie and Jane are friends of mine. Come out. *Please*."

"Leardrim!" Brodie laughed so much that snot came down his nose and he had to fumble in his pyjama pocket for his inhaler. "What kind o' a name's that?"

"Shut up!" Kirsty pushed Brodie out of the way. "You're scaring him."

She moved along the rows of sweet jars, reading the labels as she went: *Cola Cubes, Sherbet Lemons, Old-fashioned Humbugs, Exploding Fizzers, Extra-hot Peppermints, Dynamite Double Lollies.* Her gaze dropped to a large box of Mrs Sookhard's hand-made sweets which sat on the bottom shelf: *'Sookhard's' Extra-long-lasting Almost Indestructible Rock, Super-Soor Cavity Crunchers*, and *'Sick-making' Liquorice Treats.* She screwed up her face at the sight of the black liquorice spiders, beetles and bluebottles.

"What…what's that?"

Kirsty turned to see Jane standing by her side. Her mouth was wide open and she was pointing to one of the half-empty sweet jars beside the window.

"There you are!" Kirsty stared at Leardrim, who was sitting on top of a mound of cola cubes; his eyes were closed, his knees were pulled up around his ears and his nose and lips were squashed against the front of the glass bottle.

As soon as Kirsty put a hand on the jar, there was a loud *swooshing* sound and he was gone. She followed the noise and the bright light which flew around the shop before disappearing into a cardboard box of giant lollipops. A yellow lolly began to glow in the dark and she could see Leardrim's face imprinted on its sticky surface. She pulled it out of the box, screaming as it shattered into a thousand pieces. There was another loud *swoosh* and she knew that Leardrim was hiding again.

"Look!" Brodie pointed up at a huge stick of plastic rock that was suspended from the low ceiling by two brass chains.

"Please come down." Kirsty strained to look above her: Leardrim's face was set in the end of the rock, the words '*Welcome To Weerdee*' framing his features. His webbed feet were sticking out from the other end and his purple heart shone through the red and blue stripes.

"Help me with this," she said, dragging Mrs Sookhard's wobbly stepladder into the middle of the floor.

Kirsty was one step away from the top when: *SWOOSH. SWOOSH. SWOOSH. SWOOSH.* Her head twisted from side to side as she followed the luminous ball. She watched as Leardrim's terrified face appeared on almost every surface in the shop before finally disappearing.

"Where's he gone now?" asked Jane.

"Sshh." Kirsty pressed a finger against her lips and peered into the darkness: there was no sign of Leardrim anywhere.

"He jist vanished," said Brodie, shrugging his shoulders and looking like he couldn't quite believe what he'd seen. "Gone. Vamooshed. Evaporated into thin air."

"Quiet!" Kirsty moved around the shop, opening drawers and cupboards.

"Anyone fancy a free lolly?" Brodie ran towards the freezer and tugged at the sliding doors. "It's stuck," he said. "Frozen solid."

"One. Two. Three. PUSH!" Jane helped him pull back the glass door.

Kirsty joined her friends, shivering as white clouds of cold air rose into the darkness. She peered down at the leaning towers of ice-cream tubs and different kinds of icicles.

"AAAAARGH!" They all screamed at the same time.

Leardrim was lying on his back in the middle of a pile of ice poles and lollies. His small body was shaking and his eyes were staring straight ahead. The purple heart inside his chest was beating very slowly and he didn't seem to be breathing.

Chapter Eleven

Into the Lair

"Leardrim!" Kirsty pushed her hands into the chilly depths of the freezer and pulled the frozen body to the surface. She slipped off her dressing-gown and draped it over Leardrim's soft shoulders. His skin made a loud crackling noise as she put her arms around him and hugged him.

"That's revoltin'!" Brodie backed away, pulling Jane with him.

Kirsty let out a sigh of relief when she heard Leardrim cough. He lifted his head and blinked his pink eyes.

"Are you okay?" She held him at arm's length and gave him a little shake. He gave her a toothless smile before glancing nervously at Brodie and Jane.

"It's okay. You can trust them." Kirsty stroked his hand. "They won't tell."

Brodie and Jane looked terrified and shook their heads in agreement.

"I…I have to get something." Leardrim's hands trembled as he reached inside his leafy green and purple toga and pulled out a tiny silver casket. "I can't survive for long in darkness - I need the light to live."

Kirsty watched as he opened the box. A lavender-coloured light streamed out, covering his head and shoulders. He opened his mouth and took a deep breath, smiling and stretching his arms and legs as the brightness disappeared inside his body.

"Feeling better?" Kirsty smiled.

"Like new." He stood up and shook himself.

"Who are ye?" asked Brodie, moving closer.

"*What* are ye?" Jane followed, holding tightly to the sleeve of Brodie's blue-and-white striped pyjamas.

"Come into the back of the shop." Leardrim crooked a finger at Brodie and then at Jane. He turned towards Kirsty then tapped the small square of skin on his nose. "I think it's time your friends knew all about the 'Flumphaderries and Flanganans'."

"Are you sure that's a good idea?" she asked, beginning to feel even more scared than she had before.

"You said I could trust them," said Leardrim, pushing Brodie and Jane into the storeroom. "You stay here and keep a lookout."

Kirsty watched the door close behind them. She dropped to her knees and crawled towards the window.

"Oh no!" She felt her eyes widen as she peeped over the edge of the windowsill: Miss Knowall, Mrs Sookhard, Mrs Hardpiece and Mr Savage were standing in the middle of the village square, the street lights casting a yellow glow on their faces. She shuddered as she remembered the hideous creatures that were hidden under their human disguises.

She held her breath as the headmistress and the shopkeepers crossed the street and went into '*Savage's The Butcher*'. When they came out, Mr Savage was holding a big serving dish of raw steaks. Blood drip-dripped onto the pavement, leaving a trail of dark spots behind them as they walked along to the '*Rumbly Tum*' tearoom.

Gristle the pot-bellied pig pushed his head out of the café door. He was chained to Mrs Sookhard's rusty pram and he grunted as Mrs Hardpiece kicked him out of the way. He shot back inside and ran around and around, with the baby sitting up in the pram, laughing like a lunatic. Mrs Hardpiece stood aside and let her three friends file into the tearoom.

The door slammed and the Flanganans sat down at one of the gingham-covered tables.

Kirsty climbed up and knelt on the sweet shop's wide windowsill. Her breath made a misty mark on the glass as she watched Mrs Hardpiece get up and disappear into the café's kitchen, then come running back out with plates of the raw steak. She shuddered and felt sick when she saw them pick up the meat with their bare hands and bite into it. They laughed as they chewed, blood running down their chins.

"Kirsty!"

Kirsty spun around to see Leardrim standing in the doorway of the storeroom.

"M...M...Mr Savage," she said, pointing a shaking finger towards the tearoom, "and Mrs Knowall and - "

"Over here!" Leardrim sounded impatient. "You won't believe what I've found."

Kirsty blinked as she looked around the store: Brodie and Jane were huddled together in a corner and Leardrim was standing in front of a huge pile of cardboard boxes, crates and paper packing cases. A thick white candle spluttered in the darkness, casting black shadows that danced around the walls.

"Come in!" He lit another candle and pushed it into her hand. "And shut the door."

Kirsty gulped; even though the storeroom was almost in darkness, the light from the candle was bright enough to allow her to see what looked like four giant pea pods hanging from the wall. She raised her eyes and looked up at them: they were green and black with oozing yellow crusts and reminded her of a chrysalis that she'd seen in a school library book.

"Take a better look," urged Leardrim, pushing her closer.

"What…what are they?" Kirsty walked slowly towards the wall.

"Give me your hand." Leardrim pressed her fingers against one of the pods.

"Yuck!" Revulsion swept through her body as she touched the pod's crusty casing. It felt disgusting - dry and dusty with a soggy yellow edge.

"It feels warm and…and like it's breathing," said Kirsty, bringing her other hand up to explore the scaly surface.

"It is." Leardrim leaned forward and pulled away a piece of the pod's skin. "It's alive."

Kirsty's mouth dropped open as lips, a nose and two closed eyes appeared under the crusty flap. She watched as Leardrim moved along the pods, uncovering another three sleeping faces as he went.

"They look human," said Kirsty, wiping her sweating palms on her dressing-gown.

"They are. And if I'm not mistaken, inside these," he said, tapping each of the pods in turn, "are the headmaster of Weerdee Primary School and the rightful owners of the sweet shop, the butcher's and the tearoom."

"What's happened to them?"

"Remember the sticky substance that Gananzzer used to trap Elvira, Charlie and Roanna before he turned them to stone?"

Kirsty nodded.

"Well, that's what Flanganans have done to these poor souls," said Leardrim sadly. "These people have been captured and are being kept here in a kind of deep sleep state."

"It's all beginning to make sense." Kirsty held her head in her hands. "Aunt Flora told me that all the shopkeepers and the headmaster had moved away at the same time...and none of them left a forwarding address."

"It all fits," said Leardrim. "Nacnud and I suspected that the new faces in Weerdee were all Flanganans, we just haven't been able to prove it - until tonight."

"So what do we do now?" Kirsty stared at the four pods. "Do you really think that the Flanganans are going to come to the Village Fair?"

"I'm convinced of it," said Leardrim, rubbing his hands together nervously. "When the headmistress and the new shopkeepers offered to organise and sponsor the whole event, I just knew that was the day they were planning to come above ground and take over Weerdee. The signs are everywhere: people mysteriously disappearing, the dead heather, the sightings of strange insects and animals, the water pollution, the bad smells, the creeping mist that's covering the countryside - they're coming, there's no doubt about it."

"But why have they waited for so long?"

"Who knows," said Leardrim, with a sigh. "The workings of their evil minds are a mystery."

Kirsty turned towards Brodie and Jane: Jane looked like she'd been crying and Brodie's eyes were wide with fear behind his glasses.

"It's going to be okay." She crossed the storeroom and dropped to her knees beside her friends.

"Yer wee pal there." Brodie pointed at Leardrim. "He's told us...everything."

"Everything," repeated Jane. "An' we can hardly believe it - it's like a bad dream."

"It's no dream." Leardrim's webbed feet slapped against the floor as he joined them. "It's a real life, wide-awake nightmare, and we need to know if you're on our side. You must be brave and you have to promise to keep all this information to yourselves."

"Count me in." Brodie pulled his inhaler from his pyjama pocket and took two puffs.

"Me too," said Jane, managing a smile.

"Give me your green-guard." Leardrim poked a purple finger at the pocket of Kirsty's dressing-gown. "Quickly!"

"You mean my moss-ball?" she said, pulling out the spongy shell.

Leardrim laid the green-guards on the stone floor and pressed his hands on top of them. A lavender light began to form around his fingers and Kirsty watched, mesmerized, as the two multiplied and became four.

"How did ye do that?" Brodie and Jane spoke at the same time.

"Just put them on." Leardrim stuck his head through the shop's back door before climbing into his own disguise. "Come on! There's something I want to show you."

The green-guards seemed to have a life of their own, and Kirsty rolled effortlessly through the door with Brodie and Jane coming behind. She followed Leardrim, keeping close to the side of the road. A car's headlights appeared in the mist. It came speeding towards them and they all huddled together on the grass verge until it had passed and disappeared into the village.

They turned around and around in seemingly endless circles until Leardrim cried, "Stop!"

Kirsty looked through the crack in her green-guard: they were standing at the bottom of Bennachie. The 'Mither Tap' towered above them, dark and jagged against the sky.

"Stay right behind me," instructed Leardrim. "And don't leave the path."

Kirsty drew her knees up tightly under her chin as they began to travel up the mountain track. Her gasps and groans joined Brodie and Jane's as they bounced over sharp sticks and stones and trundled over the tangled roots of trees. The spicy scent of evergreens mingled with the smell of damp earth and an owl hoot-hooted in the darkness.

"Why are we stopping here?" Kirsty joined Leardrim, who was circling the entrance to Hosie's Well.

"It'll soon be daylight," he whispered, looking up at the stripes of pink and apricot that were beginning to brighten the sky. "Come on! There's something I want you to see."

Kirsty felt her heartbeat quicken as Leardrim moved his green-guard to the edge of the pool of water. She peered down into the well, trying to see the dividing wall that she'd found on her first visit to Bennachie. One side glowed with a pale lilac light and the other was green and cloudy with ribbons of foul-smelling yellow smoke rising from its surface.

"Leave your green-guards there." Leardrim pointed to a big boulder. "Then hold your nose and jump in. And remember - it's the left-hand side."

Kirsty heard the splash as Leardrim, Jane and then Brodie plunged into the murky depths. She held her breath as she followed them, dropping through a wall of water before landing on her feet on a slippery stone step.

Leardrim offered Kirsty his hand and helped her onto a long staircase that stretched as far as she could see. "I'll go first," he said. "Then you, Brodie, and then Jane. Kirsty," he added, his mouth looking like a black hole in the darkness, "you stay at the back."

Kirsty pressed the palms of her hands against the sides of the narrow passageway. The walls were running with water and drips landed on her forehead and ran down to the end of her nose. She tried not to slip on the moss-covered steps as she walked along in near-darkness, only able to see her feet by the ghostly green glow that rose from the blackness below.

"Everybody keep perfectly quiet." Leardrim dropped to his knees as he reached the end of the staircase. "Lie down on your stomachs and crawl behind me. And don't make a single sound."

Kirsty's nails dug into a thick layer of moss as they stopped moving and looked down into a deep dark hole. She felt dizzy as she stared into the rocky crater. A stomach-turning stink filled her nose and she could see the same green mist she'd noticed hovering just above the ground on Bennachie.

Kirsty gave a gasp of astonishment as the haze cleared. An animal skin with a crudely-drawn map of Weerdee painted on it swung from two giant hooks. Hundreds of horrible creatures hung upside down like big black bats, while others lay face down on nests of heather, moss and twigs. Flickering flames burned against the walls, casting their light on ropes of sticky black slime, animal skulls, and bones strewn everywhere.

Gananzzer was asleep in front of a roaring red fire and Vasveegal snored on a fat velvet cushion, a sticky stream of saliva running from his great slack mouth.

"So this is where the Flanganans are hiding," whispered Kirsty.

"I think we should get oot o' here," said Brodie, pulling on Jane's sleeve.

"Aye," said Jane, looking back at the stone staircase, "before someone or *something* comes doon those steps."

"Don't worry, they should all be asleep," said Leardrim. "Flanganans usually return to their lair long before dawn and sleep till night falls again."

"I want to go too," said Kirsty. "I'm scared."

"I just wanted you all to see what we're dealing with," said Leardrim. "Now let's get back up to the top."

Kirsty felt faint with fear as they trooped along a shadowy tunnel with Leardrim leading the way, his blue brain shining like a light bulb. A labyrinth of smaller passages branched off from the main corridor and with every one they passed safely, she breathed a sigh of relief.

"I dinna think that I can go on for much longer," said Brodie, holding his chest and wheezing.

"Me neither," gasped Jane, slumping against the wall.

"Come on," pleaded Kirsty. "You can't just stop. *Ugh!*" She screwed up her face and sniffed. "It smells like a zoo in here. What is that?"

"Oh no!" Leardrim covered his nose with a hand. "I'd forgotten about the Podasks."

"What...what's a Podask?" Kirsty screamed as three long-legged beasts that looked like small, feathered dinosaurs came flying towards them.

"They're the gate guards!" cried Leardrim, his own wings appearing from his back. "Quickly! Brodie and Jane, give me your hands. Kirsty! You hold onto my feet."

Kirsty kept her head down as they rose to the roof, then flew up the tunnel at an incredible speed. The Podasks were coming close behind, their wings flapping. Their eyes were bloodshot and bulging and their pointed brown teeth chattered up and down. She kicked her feet out as they gnashed and snapped at her bare heels.

Kirsty ducked as Leardrim suddenly dropped down and disappeared under a gap in a small door.

"Give me a hand to get this closed!" He clambered to his feet as soon as they hit the soft earth.

Kirsty crawled across and helped Leardrim, while Brodie and Jane kicked away the sharp yellow claws that scraped at the ground.

"That was a close escape." Leardrim pressed his back against the dividing door, his purple heart fluttering inside his chest. The rows of bubbles that travelled around his body danced as if they had reached boiling point. His tiny chest heaved and his brain blubbered around inside his head.

Kirsty looked up and saw they were sitting in a narrow earth-walled tunnel.

"It's the way out." Leardrim smiled and nodded towards a wooden ladder that swung against the wall. "You go first."

The rungs on the ladder were made from ropes of pleated heather and creaked and groaned as Kirsty began to climb. She could hear the scratching sounds of the Podasks' claws against the door and smell the wet soil next to her face. Worms squeezed out through the earth; wood lice and creepy-crawlies that her mum called 'Forty-Footed Jinnys' ran across her cheeks and tickled at the corners of her mouth.

"Come on, you two. Let's get out of here." Leardrim called to Brodie and Jane. "CLIMB!"

The first light of day was beginning to shine through a crack in the tunnel's ceiling. Leardrim reached over Kirsty's head and banged his fist against it. On the third knock it gave way. They all screamed when they saw the dark figure who was looking down on them.

Chapter Twelve

Through the Heather Hatch

"I've been lookin' all over the place for ye!" cried Flora, folding her fat arms across her wobbly body. "I woke up an' ye'd jist vanished."

Kirsty almost cried with relief as her aunt's red hands reached down into the tunnel and pulled her out. Scarlet, was parked on the path; Kirsty let out a long sigh as she slumped against the side-car and looked around. They'd come back up to the surface just under the summit of the 'Mither Tap', on the opposite side of the path from Hosie's Well.

"How many more o' ye are doon there?" Flora's huge backside swayed in the air as she held back the small hatch in the heather and hauled Leardrim, Brodie and Jane to the surface.

"What do ye think ye're doin'?" Flora thumped Leardrim on the arm. "Are ye mad?"

"Someone had to show her what we're up against," he said, standing up and dusting the dirt from his clothes. "And as for these two," he nodded towards Brodie and Jane, "they just sort of got involved."

"I'd planned to tell her myself this morning," said Flora, stamping down the heather hatch with her big boots. "I was jist waitin' for the right time."

"Time's something we don't have," said Leardrim. "The Fair's today."

"As if I'm likely to forget." Flora looked at Leardrim and then at Kirsty, before asking, "How much does she know?"

"Almost everything," he whispered.

Kirsty was wondering what Leardrim meant by, '*almost everything*' when he began to glow and vibrate. Slowly, his face and body changed back into those of Hosie the cat.

Brodie and Jane sat in stunned silence as the transformation became complete.

"We've known each other a long time, but Flora still prefers me in my feline form," laughed Hosie, waving his tail in the air.

Kirsty pulled on Flora's spare crash helmet and jumped onto Scarlet's pillion seat. Jane and Brodie squeezed into the side-car and Hosie balanced on top of the headlight as they rode off down the mountain path, only stopping to pick up their green-guards, before taking the road which led into Weerdee.

She held on tightly to Flora, Scarlet's exhaust backfiring and belching out clouds of black fumes as they went. The residents of Weerdee were still asleep, their curtains closed, bottles of milk standing on their doorsteps like little white soldiers.

Scarlet climbed up the through the village, whizzing past trees and hedges on the way back to Benderrie Manor. The moss-covered statues in the woods on one side of the road seemed to stare after them as they roared along to meet the circle of standing stones on the other.

Kirsty removed her crash helmet as Scarlet spluttered to a standstill outside the big house. Hosie leapt down from the bike and raced up to the front door, transforming himself back into Leardrim as he landed on the top step.

"This place looks even more massive close up," said Jane, opening the door of the side-car.

"Humungous," added Brodie.

"Get inside!" Flora attempted to tidy her red hair with her hands. "We've got things we need to discuss and we haven't got much time."

"What's happened here?" Kirsty gasped as she looked around: the entrance hall was even dirtier than before and all her Great-Grandfather's hunting trophies were almost hidden under a thick layer of grime.

"I think we've had visitors." Flora sighed and rolled a ball of dust between her fat fingers. "The Flanganans used to be afraid to come above ground. They were scared o' this," she said, pulling out the silver key that hung around her neck. "But lately they've been gettin' braver an' braver."

"Do you think they've guessed where the book is hidden?" asked Kirsty.

"Well, they know it's somewhere in the house." Flora lowered her voice. "And ever since I put the book back under the rocker, that room's never been at peace. It sometimes sounds like a war zone in there."

Like a battle between good and evil, thought Kirsty, remembering Leardrim's words. She shuddered as her bare feet made a sucking sound against the floor: something sticky had covered the tiles and the banister that wound its way to the upper floors of the house.

"Let's take a look in here." Flora put an arm around Brodie and Jane, guiding them through the stone archway and into the picture gallery.

"These are the kids who opened the book," she said, pointing at the painting of herself and her sisters.

"I recognize you," said Brodie, "but which one's Elvira?"

Jane moved closer and peered at the painting.

"That's her there," said Kirsty, jabbing a finger into the canvas. She stared at the picture: everything was just as it had been and the book was still on Elvira's lap.

"We meet again," said a voice from the end of the gallery.

"Nacnud!" Kirsty smiled as Leardrim's companion joined them.

"Why did she have to do it?" He shook his head sadly and touched Elvira's painted face.

"It's what we can do to make things right that matters now," said Leardrim, coming up the steps to meet them. "Everyone here's aware of the facts, so let's get on with making plans to save Weerdee and to get you and me back where we belong."

Kirsty, Leardrim, Nacnud, Flora, Brodie and Jane sat facing each other around Benderrie Manor's enormous kitchen table.

"Maybe we could call an emergency public meeting," suggested Jane.

"Are ye mad?" Brodie blinked hard behind his glasses.

"Who'd believe us anyway?" said Kirsty, giving a nervous laugh.

"No!" Nacnud looked panic-stricken and rested his bald head on his arms. "We can't discuss this with anybody."

"Absolutely, totally, nobody," said Leardrim. "If the Flanganans know that we suspect them, we may lose our chance of recapturing them forever - we have to take them by surprise."

Nacnud raised his head and nodded in agreement. "We'll all go to the Fair together and Flora will hide the book under her clothes until we're satisfied that all the Flanganans are above ground. Nobody must do or say *anything* until either Leardrim or I say so."

"And if everything goes according to plan," added Leardrim, "the Flanganans will soon be back under lock and key and Nacnud and I will be on our way home."

"Din odack bi normo," said Nacnud, reaching across the table and covering one of Leardrim's three-fingered hands with his own.

Their purple hearts glowed in their chests as they touched.

"Gi norbano." Sparkling tears raced down Leardrim's face then bounced off the table and onto the floor.

"What *are* you saying?" asked Kirsty.

"I must apologize." Leardrim smiled. "We lapsed back into Derrish when we thought about going home."

"You speak two languages!" said Kirsty.

"We used our advanced technology to tune into your speech frequency," said Nacnud, pointing at the base of his brain. "We can unscramble and decode any form of communication."

"Wow!" said Brodie and Jane at the same time.

"I think we should get back to the immediate problem." Flora slapped the palms of her hands against the table. "It's nearly mornin' an' the Fair's at two o'clock this afternoon." She got up and pulled a big black bin liner from a cupboard. She nodded at Leardrim and Nacnud before saying, "I've jist thought o' a way that ye can mingle with the crowds without havin' to transform."

Kirsty watched as Flora emptied a bag of old clothes onto the floor.

"I collect jumble for my craft and design work," she said, dropping to her knees and rooting through the brightly coloured cast-offs. "I'm sure that we'll find somethin' in here to suit you two."

Five minutes later, Nacnud and Leardrim were dressed in jogging bottoms, old trainers and long-sleeved rugby shirts with the collars turned up to hide their faces. Baseball caps and two pairs of Kirsty's wrap-around sunglasses completed their disguises.

"You look great," said Brodie.

"Almost human," agreed Jane.

"Right then!" Flora looked up at the grandfather clock in the corner of the kitchen. "I think I should get you two home before someone gets up and discovers you're gone."

Kirsty, Leardrim and Nacnud followed Flora as she put her arms around Brodie and Jane and steered them into the entrance hall and out through the front door.

"We'll meet you outside the Fair at five minutes to two," shouted Leardrim.

"Don't be late." Nacnud lifted his silver shades and smiled after them.

"They'll be there," said Kirsty, sounding more confident than she felt.

Suddenly a muffled thumping and clattering that she knew was coming from the forbidden bedroom made her turn and look up: a thick rope of green smoke twisted around the banister for a moment before taking the shape of a yellow snake with a huge, flat head. Its forked tongue flicked in and out and it stared at them for a moment before disappearing back up the stairs.

"Don't look," said Leardrim, closing the heavy oak door and slipping a comforting arm around her waist. "It's only an illusion - the Flanganans are trying to confuse and scare us."

"Then it's working. I'm not even sure what's real and what's my imagination anymore," said Kirsty, resting her forehead against the window.

The thought of going to the Fair made worry worms wriggle in her stomach as she watched her Aunt Flora roar down the drive on Scarlet, with Brodie hanging onto her leather jacket and Jane in the side-car.

Chapter Thirteen

Weerdee Fair

Kirsty kept her head down and tried not to look at Mr Savage as she waited by the turnstile with Flora, Leardrim and Nacnud. The butcher's bald head was shiny with sweat and she could see the dirt under his long fingernails as he raked the entrance money into a rusty red biscuit tin. She looked at her watch: it was just after two o'clock and hundreds of people were already streaming into Weerdee's village park.

The sun was shining and a pipe band was playing.

"I hope Brodie and Jane haven't said anythin' to anybody," said Flora, adjusting the front of the huge pink knickers that concealed the Book of Bennachie.

"I told you before!" Kirsty shouted over the noise of the pipes and drums. "You can trust them."

"Here they are." Leardrim jumped up and down impatiently.

"Oh no! They're not on their own," said Nacnud.

"See ye later!" Brodie waved at his parents as he ran towards Kirsty.

"We made it," gasped Jane. "We told Brodie's Mam an' Dad an' my Auntie Nell that we wanted to look round the Fair by ourselves."

"Right, let's go, an' dinna draw attention to yerselves." Flora pushed everyone into the queue.

"One adult an' five children," she said, slapping her money into Mr Savage's hand.

They all held their breath and looked away as Mr Savage eyed Flora suspiciously before counting the heads and nodding for them to go in.

"Just keep walking," hissed Kirsty, not daring to look back, even when Flora's big behind became stuck in the wooden turnstile.

After a short struggle, Flora was free. Red-faced and gasping for breath, she caught up with them outside the hot dog stand.

"If we want to blend in," she puffed, sniffing at the delicious smells that were wafting through the air, "I think we'd better have somethin' to eat."

Five minutes later, Kirsty, Brodie and Jane were tucking into extra-large hot dogs with juicy fried onions and tomato ketchup. Flora bought three huge candy flosses on sticks. Leardrim and Nacnud used the sticky pink clouds to hide their faces while Flora tucked greedily into hers, making funny little grunting noises as she ate.

"What will we do first?" Kirsty wiped sauce from her chin and looked around the park.

"Nothing," said Nacnud. "There's nothing we *can* do until we're sure that Vasveegal, Gananzzer and all the Flanganans have come above ground. Remember what I told you - "

"They all have to be in the same place at the same time before you can try to turn the key and recapture them," interrupted Kirsty.

Nacnud nodded. "We'll have a good scout round, keeping our eyes and ears open. And don't forget," he said, squinting out from behind his shades, "some of the more unusual sights you'll see here this afternoon won't be real. They're only illusions which have been conjured up by the Flanganans for the Fair."

"Whatever happens," said Leardrim, pulling the collar of his striped rugby shirt up around his chin, "we must all stick together."

Kirsty stared in amazement as they walked around the Fair. One half of the showground was filled with blaring pop music, colourful carnival rides, sales stalls and burger vans, and the other was devoted to something called '*Wally Wamboozle's Would-Ya-Believe-It? Weird And Wacky Freakshow*'.

"I thought freakshows were banned nowadays," said Kirsty, turning to Leardrim and shouting over the noise. A red and gold fairground organ was playing by itself, its keys moved up and down by invisible fingers. "It's like something from Victorian times."

"What did Nacnud tell you?" He put a hand on her arm.

"It's only an illusion," she whispered.

"That's right. Flanganans have no conscience and anything they choose to show you will be designed to shock."

"Only an illusion," repeated Kirsty, as they walked in silence around the circle of five open-fronted trailers.

'*X-Ray Sam - The World's Skinniest Man. (See every bone in his body)*' said the hand-painted sign which hung above the first trailer. Kirsty held her breath when a bald man came out from behind a blue velvet curtain. He stood sideways and when he breathed in, his ribs touched his backbone and you could see the outline of his heart beating beneath his skin.

'*Maritime Maisie - The Sea's Ugliest Mermaid.*' The next set of red and gold lettering was wet and shiny; Kirsty screwed up her face as a strong smell of fish filled the air. She covered her nose with the sleeve of her jumper and stared at the mermaid who was lying on a dripping tarpaulin stretched out in front of a cardboard cut-out seashore. Maisie's shimmering blue tail slapped against the black plastic and her waist-length hair was draped across her features and upper body. Every few seconds, she pushed back her golden mane to reveal the face of a wrinkled old sea-hag with bulging fish eyes and a thick-lipped fish grin.

'*The Tiny Family*' said the third sign. Kirsty bent down and peered through one of the upstairs windows of what looked like an enormous doll's house. She gasped when she saw what was inside: six tiny trolls were sitting drinking tea from little cups and saucers. Suddenly, the tallest troll got up from his chair, stuck his hairy hand through the window and grabbed her nose. He gave it a good hard pinch before appearing at the front door of his home and shouting, "Clear off, kid! Don't you know it's rude to stare?"

Kirsty rubbed her nose as they moved on to the fourth trailer: the biggest baby she had ever seen was sitting on a play-mat. It had a placard around its neck that said '*Kid Colossal, The Planet's Tallest, Heaviest, Windiest Baby*'.

"Oh my!" Flora gathered everyone in front of her like a protective mother hen with a brood of chicks. "Would ye believe that?"

Kirsty couldn't believe it and Brodie and Jane stood in stunned silence.

The baby held a big bottle of milk in one fat-knuckled hand and a huge rattle in the other. He wore nothing but a massive towelling nappy with a gigantic rusty safety pin. They watched as a blob of drool blubbered on his bottom lip for a moment before dropping to the ground and splashing them.

"Yuck!" cried everyone at the same time. And then, when they were all wiping their faces on their sleeves, the baby opened its mouth and did the biggest, whiffiest burp that any of them had ever heard or smelt before. They all gagged as the wind blew the hair back from their faces.

"Let's go," said Flora, pushing everyone towards the next exhibit.

Kirsty curled up her nose in disgust at the animal smells that were coming from the biggest trailer on the show-field.

'*Wally Wamboozle's World Famous Amazing Animal Zoo.*' Kirsty read the banner that fluttered in the breeze. Below it was a collection of some of the most bizarre beasts she had ever seen. The unfortunate creatures were chained together by the ankles and stood in a line, shuffling their feet in the straw.

"ROLL UP! ROLL UP! See some of the world's strangest animals!"

They all moved back when a dwarf dressed like a circus ring-master jumped up through a hatch in the trailer's wooden floor.

"Marvel at Dalruble, the dancing dog," he said, pulling at the droopy ears of a sad-faced hound that wore shiny black shoes and went rat-a-tap-tat in time to the music from a Victorian organ. "See the Bunniphant!" He pointed at a wrinkly elephant with a buck-toothed rabbit's head. "Laugh at the two-headed horse with the cow's udder," he shouted, prodding at the poor beast with the end of his whip.

The dwarf removed his black top hat with a flourish and said, "May I introduce the star of our show - GUNELLA! The piano-playing Gorilla."

Kirsty felt horrified when she saw Gunella's big brown eyes turn to look at her from under a curly blonde wig. She was wearing red lipstick, frosted blue eye shadow and a green and white dress with matching frilly bloomers.

Her hands flew across the keys, big diamond rings flashing on every finger. And her feet, squashed into high-heeled silver shoes, moved up and down on the piano's pedals.

"I love animals!" Kirsty covered her eyes with her hands. "I can't bear to see them being treated like this."

"Remember what Nacnud told you?" whispered Leardrim, moving to stand by her side. "None of this is real. It's all the work of the Flanganans: they've taken the worst nightmares of decent people and made them come alive. Come on! We've got to move on." He took her hand and pulled her through the crowds towards the enormous black marquee that stood just beyond the trailers.

'Unveiled To The Public At 3.30. For A Limited Time Only: VASVEEGAL - The Gigantic, Smelly, Jelly Monster' said the banner which hung on the front of the tent.

"It's ten past three now," said Flora, pushing her hands inside her skirt and hoisting up her voluminous pink pants. "Not long to wait until - what on earth?"

She let her knicker elastic snap back with a loud crack as they all turned and looked towards the other end of the show park: a terrible commotion was coming from the direction of the carnivals.

Chapter Fourteen

The Guardian

"Wow! It's massive." Kirsty rocked on her heels as she stared up at the red and yellow pirate ship ride that had appeared in the middle of the park: it was as long as a football pitch and had rows and rows of wooden seats.

"ROLL UP! ROLL UP! Free admission for all you lucky guys and gals. We can't start the ride until all the seats are full." A frighteningly familiar voice boomed out over the loud music.

Kirsty swallowed and looked up to see Gananzzer, the horrible creature who had made the deal with Elvira. He was wearing a pirate outfit, with a patch across one eye, a red-and-white spotted scarf knotted around his scrawny neck, and a black skull and crossbones hat. The ugly beast was standing at the bow of the ship, his hairy arms stretched wide to reach the ropes that were attached to the gigantic creamy-coloured sails.

"What's *she* up to?" Flora poked Kirsty in the ribs and pointed to where Mrs Sookhard stood holding a big baking tray, piled high with squares of toffee.

"Leardrim," whispered Kirsty, "that looks like the tray that the Flanganans were pouring the spit-stuff into."

"What spit-stuff?" asked Brodie and Jane.

"Sssh!" Kirsty pressed a finger against her lips and turned her attention to the pirate ship: nearly all the seats were already full and the queue was almost at an end.

"A free sample of '*Sookhard's Special Recipe Toffee*' for everyone who rides the Pirate Ship," cried the sweetshop owner. Her baby was sitting up in its rusty pram with a toffee apple in one hand and a big bag of chips in the other.

A snuffling noise made Kirsty turn around: Gristle was grunting and slobbering, his studded collar glinting in the sunlight. Mrs Hardpiece gave him a kick and turned to smile at Miss Knowall and Mr Savage; they were standing in front of a big group of strange-looking people who were making no attempt to get on the ride.

"All those people on the ship must be locals or visitors who have come for the Fair." Kirsty shivered, a trickle of sweat running down her back. "And everyone behind us," she said, jerking a thumb towards the crowd at her back, "I think they're-"

"Flanganans," interrupted Flora.

VOOM-VOOM. The ride began to rock, slowly at first, then faster and faster.

VOOM-VOOM. The noise seemed to swell to fill the air.

"SCREAM!" Gananzzer screeched with laughter, before disappearing in a cloud of green smoke. "Scream if ye wanna go faster."

But although the passengers' eyes were bulging with fear, they couldn't scream. Their mouths worked frantically, their teeth and lips stuck together by the special recipe toffee.

VOOM-VOOM-VOOM. The pirate ship was moving so quickly now that its bright colours and the faces of the riders were just a blur.

"It's almost half past three!" yelled Brodie, pointing at his watch.

"Let's go!" Flora turned and bolted down the park with Kirsty, Leardrim, Nacnud, Brodie and Jane running behind her.

They arrived outside Vasveegal's tent just in time to see Gananzzer tugging out the pegs with both of his gnarled hands.

"Get ready!" Leardrim bellowed at Flora. "Give Kirsty the key."

"No!" Kirsty felt terrified when Flora pulled the book out of her pink knickers, ripped the chain from her neck then pressed the key into her hand. "Leardrim only said that he needed my help, he didn't say that *I* had to turn the key. If the official Guardian can't do it, then I think it should be either him or Nacnud."

"But you *are* the Guardian!" Flora shouted to be heard above the terrible noise from the pirate ship and the ferocious gale that was whipping up around them. "Elvira an' Charlie had *two* babies - twin daughters. And you, Kirsty," she held her by the shoulders and shook her until her teeth rattled, "were the first-born by fifteen minutes. On the afternoon that Gananzzer came back to remind Elvira of her promise, you were in another room with me. An' on the day that yer poor family was turned to stone, you were safe at the Manor with Harriet."

"You mean, Elvira and Charlie are my *parents* and Harriet is really my auntie?" Kirsty felt her head begin to whirl in confusion. "So...so Roanna is my sister. No. No! It *can't* be true."

"It's true! Every word. That's why we persuaded Harriet to take you with her when she moved down to London: we couldn't risk Gananzzer finding out about you."

Kirsty covered her ears with both hands as the *vooming* noise became louder and louder.

They all looked up just in time to see the pirate ship break free from its axle and fly through the air. It spun round and round above their heads before disappearing into the distance.

And then an indescribably awful smell made them all turn around to face the circus tent: Gananzzer was tugging at the last peg and green smoke was billowing into the air.

"TURN IT!" cried Nacnud. "Turn the key back around."

Kirsty's hand trembled as her fingers closed around the key. She glanced over her shoulder; Miss Knowall and the shopkeepers were marching towards her, followed by the pack of peculiar people. Gristle was running alongside Mrs Sookhard and her baby, who was sitting up in its pram as it trundled down the hill.

"TURN IT!" roared Leardrim.

And Kirsty was just about to when Gristle came thundering towards her. She screamed as the pot-bellied porker hit her hard in the chest, knocking the key out of her hand and straight into his open mouth. He grunted twice, swallowed it, then took off like a rocket towards the carnivals. Kirsty pushed the Book of Bennachie inside her jacket and grabbed the end of Gristle's chain; he pulled her along the ground, protesting loudly, with Flora, Leardrim, Nacnud, Brodie and Jane racing behind.

Gristle ran around in a circle before stopping at a stall selling multi-coloured helium balloons.

POP. POP. POP. He sunk his teeth into balloon after balloon and Kirsty looked on in amazement as he began to float up into the air, his belly blowing up until he looked like a huge black football.

Kirsty took a step back as Gristle made a farting noise and then exploded with a loud bang. She watched as the shiny silver key fell through the air and landed in her hand.

"NOooo!" howled Miss Knowall, as Kirsty pulled the book from her jacket and slid the key into the lock.

The shopkeepers and the crowd behind Miss Knowall skidded to a standstill. There was silence as Kirsty turned the key back around.

The racket that followed the silence was deafening. Lightning cracked, thunder rumbled and the sky grew black and angry. The exhibits from *Wally Wamboozle's* freakshow were dancing around on the grass, showers of sparks were flying from the carnival rides and fountains of brightly coloured jelly beans spewed from a sweet machine and rained down on them.

Kirsty screamed as the baby's skin split like a sausage in a pan to show a revolting rat-like creature. A terrible moaning sound was coming from Miss Knowall and her shopkeeper friends. Green smoke poured from their ears; they shrank until they were just piles of slack skin which shrivelled up to reveal four more of the terrible beasts. And then, withering and wrinkling before her eyes, the mad-eyed mob dropped to their knees and joined them.

"NO!" Gananzzer crawled towards Kirsty, followed by Vasveegal, who was becoming smaller and smaller by the second.

Kirsty kicked away Gananzzer's hands as he clawed at the book. He gave a loud groan as the eyes on the cover blinked. The mouth opened and a black, swirling tunnel rose into the air. Gananzzer picked up Vasveegal and pushed him into his pocket. He crouched on the ground and covered his head with his hands as the rest of the Flanganans were sucked into the darkness.

"You're finished!" Kirsty held the book up in front of Gananzzer and Vasveegal. They roared with anger as the spinning vortex drew them, kicking and screaming, into its black heart.

"You did it!" Leardrim and Nacnud staggered towards Kirsty and flung their arms around her.

"She did it!" panted Flora, lying flat on her back with Brodie and Jane by her side.

"It had to be me!" Kirsty's whole body shook with relief as the sun suddenly came out over Bennachie. The heather on the mountain burst into brilliant purple-blue bloom and clear sparkling water ran down its slopes and rained from the sky.

"I'm the Guardian of the book and key," she shouted, spreading her arms wide and taking in deep gulps of the crisp, clean air, "the Guardian of Bennachie!"

Chapter Fifteen

Gifts and Goodbyes

Kirsty followed Flora into the wood, branches scraping at her face and the Book of Bennachie bouncing up and down inside her jacket as she ran. She held her breath as her aunt stopped in front of the statues which stood in the clearing and began to peel away the thick layer of green moss.

Slowly, the sleeping faces of Elvira, Charlie and Roanna were revealed. Their eyelids were stuck together and slimy snail-trails of Gananzzer's glue glistened on their cheeks.

"Wake up," cried Flora, hugging her family and wiping away the tears that were rolling down her face. "Ye're free an' Kirsty's here with me!"

Kirsty jumped as Elvira's odd eyes suddenly snapped open and looked straight into her own. Baby Roanna gave a frightened cry. Charlie blinked twice then stretched out a hand.

And then a humming noise began:

"Come on! We have to go. I told Leardrim an' Nacnud that we'd meet them at the stone circle," yelled Flora, turning towards the strange sound. She grabbed Kirsty's arm and crooked a fat finger at Brodie and Jane who were watching from the edge of the clearing.

Kirsty felt as if she was dreaming as they all crossed the road. The humming noise was hurting her head and ringing in her ears as they ran towards a blinding light.

"NO!" cried Kirsty, when she saw Leardrim and Nacnud standing in front of the Channelling Stone; their arms were stretched wide and their faces were tilted skywards, the stone's purple glow radiating through their tiny bodies.

"*Please.* Don't go!" she shouted, as a diamond-shaped craft dropped silently through the clouds and hovered in the air above them, sending two beams of lilac light towards the ground.

Kirsty ran towards her Flumphaderrie friends, crying when they put their soft arms around her and held her close.

Crystal tears ran down Nacnud's face as he pulled away and looked up at her. "I want you to keep the Book of Bennachie as a symbol of the love and trust between us," he said, turning to smile at everyone. "Return it to its hiding place and keep its secret safe."

"Please accept these gifts," said Leardrim, "of healing and of flight." He pressed his purple palms against Kirsty's back, then took both her hands in his, his fingers crackling as they closed around her own.

Kirsty's whole body trembled and tingled as the lavender light which was forming around his hands disappeared into her own body.

Leardrim and Nacnud looked up as the dazzling diamond above them began to stretch and vibrate.

"Haroberd is waiting," they said together, as they stepped into the shimmering shafts.

Flora gave a loud sob and everyone wiped away tears as the bright beams lifted Leardrim and Nacnud up through an opening in the bottom of the strangely-shaped craft.

They followed the progress of the spaceship as it rose, higher and higher until it finally disappeared from sight.

*

Kirsty hugged her baby sister and thought that she would burst with happiness when her proud parents put their arms around her. She smiled across at her Aunt Flora, who stood with Brodie and Jane. She had what she'd always wanted: a family, friends, and a place that she could truly call home.

She gasped in wonder as a purple rainbow curved in the air before reaching down to where she stood, bathing her in lavender light. The gentle humming of a thousand voices rose like a heavenly choir and the wonderful scent of flowers filled the air as a smiling image of Nacnud and Leardrim appeared against the clouds.

A little shiver ran along her spine, her purple heart fluttered inside her chest and her secret wings stirred against her back. The wind sighed and the trees whispered, and way above, the great blue mountain called Bennachie smiled down on all of them.

Postscript

Extract from local newspaper: *The Inverdoorie Squawk*

'Fracas at Fair'

by
Hilary Haivers

Residents of Chapel of Weerdee got more than they bargained for when they turned out in force for the annual Village Fair.

This year's event was sponsored and organised by Weerdee's newly appointed headmistress and its shopkeepers. The most unusual spectacle of the day was the appearance of a travelling extravaganza called *'Wally Wamboozle's Would-Ya-Believe-It? Weird And Wacky Freakshow'*. Inexplicably, film of the amazing sights was found to be blank when developed.

A carnival Pirate Ship ride and its passengers went missing for over five hours before finally turning up, almost four miles away, on the roof of Inverdoorie's Town Hall.

Weerdee's headmistress and shopkeepers vanished and were immediately replaced by the old headmaster and former shop owners, who had no memory of where they had been or how they had got back.

When interviewed, residents seemed confused and unsure about what had happened at Saturday's Fair.

Latest reports are that The Ministry of Defence is investigating sightings of unexplained lights and unusually shaped aircraft above the Stone Circle at Benderrie Manor on the outskirts of Weerdee.